# TAKEN AWAY

# EHI IKE
# TAKEN AWAY

Tate Publishing & Enterprises

Published by Tate Publishing & Enterprises, LLC
127 E. Trade Center Terrace | Mustang, Oklahoma 73064 USA
1.888.361.9473 | www.tatepublishing.com

Tate Publishing is committed to excellence in the publishing industry. The company reflects the philosophy established by the founders, based on Psalm 68:11,
*"The Lord gave the word and great was the company of those who published it."*

Book design copyright © 2010 by Tate Publishing, LLC. All rights reserved.
*Cover design by Tyler Evans*
*Interior design by Lindsay B. Behrens*

Published in the United States of America

ISBN: 978-1-61566-973-8
1. Fiction / Suspense    2. Fiction / Romance / Suspense
10.02.22

# ONE

*Boom. Boom.* There was a knock on the door. I was scared to open it. My mother always told me to never open the door when she was not home. I was in the living room, sitting on the couch. The living room was ten steps away from the door.

I lived in a pretty small neighborhood in Eufaula, Alabama. The houses were not million-dollar mansions or anything like that. Just last week my neighbor was robbed. I liked living in Eufaula, Alabama, though. It was quiet most of the time.

I heard a voice from outside, but I could not quite understand what was being said. The voice sounded familiar.

I got up from the couch and took one step. *Boom.* I took another. *Boom.* Once I took the third step, the voice sounded more familiar. I could hear my heart beating more than I could hear my gasps for air. I took three more steps. Once I was at the door, I could understand what the voice was saying.

"Mimi, it's me. Open the door!"

It was just my friend Brittney. I knew I wasn't supposed to have people at my house when my mom was not home, but I opened the door anyway.

"What took you so long?" she asked.

"Sorry, I didn't know who you were," I said.

She just walked into my house and sat on the couch. Brittney was that type of person. She would just walk into your house and go into your refrigerator. Brittney's long, brown hair went perfectly with her honey-nut skin tone and oval-shaped head. She had a petite body and was short, but her personality made up for her height.

"So I have to tell you something, but first wait till Ash gets here."

Ashley was another one of my friends, but I did not invite her to my house. As a matter of fact, I didn't invite Brittney either.

"Britt, you cannot just be inviting people to my house. You know that, right? My mom is not even here, and when she sees all these people, I will be grounded!" I said furiously.

"Don't worry. Your mom loves us! She won't mind."

"What do you have to tell us?" I said.

"Don't worry. You'll find out when Ashley gets here."

Britt did not like telling stories over and over again because she would tell me and then have to tell Ashley, or the other way around. She hated doing that, so she just stuck to telling us at the same time.

Brittney turned the TV to the news channel.

"That's surprising none of you guys watch the news, except your mom every once in a while."

"Breaking news: What is going to happen to parents who earn less than $50,000 a year? Find out tonight at seven," I read from the TV.

Brittney looked at me. "Maybe they are going to give you a tax break." Brittney's parents made more money than that, but my mom didn't. We were not poor; we just did not make that much money.

"Ashley should be here by now," Britt said.

Just then there was another knock on the door.

"That must be her, but she told me she would call me first," Britt said. *Why doesn't anyone ring the doorbell!*

*Boom. Boom.* Britt got up and opened the door. Two men who looked like television FBI agents framed the doorway.

"May I help you?" Britt said. *How can she just come into my house and act like she lives here? That's just Brittney, I guess.*

One guy showed his badge as the other one spoke.

"You have to come with us. Both of you."

"Why? And how do we know those badges are real?" Britt said. Sometimes I honestly want her to shut up!

"Listen, we are taking you somewhere else, and we do not have time to play games with little ten-year-olds right now. Just be happy that you're leaving."

"Leaving what? Where are you taking us?" Without answering us, they grabbed us and shoved us into their car.

I had no idea where we were going or who they were. They did not give us any information. My mom would freak out if I was still gone when she got home. Did this have something to do with the seven o'clock news story?

Britt was still blabbing on, asking them seemingly hundreds of questions. After she had nothing else to ask, she repeated the questions she had already asked. Then she looked at me. She looked scared. Britt was never scared, but fear was written all over her face. My fear was probably clearly marked on my face as well. I whispered to Britt, "Get your phone out and text someone." She got out her phone. It didn't work. The guy in the passenger seat saw us. He took Brittney's cell phone and said, "Trying to get away? It is not going to work." Then he got duct tape and covered our mouths and blindfolded us with bandanas. Now I knew there was no way they were FBI agents. They would not be this cruel.

I was afraid. The driver kept mumbling something, but I could not worry about it. Britt was still trying to talk again. She was scared. I just closed my eyes and prayed—prayed for it to be over, prayed for my mom to be okay, and prayed for Brittney not to freak out. I just prayed.

# TWO

Finally the car stopped. Someone pulled us out of the car but kept the duct tape and bandanas on us. I couldn't tell where we were. I felt like my feet were covered in grass. We were walking. There were more people, I could tell. One of the guys was holding me tight, and I guessed the other guy was holding Brittney. They finally stopped and took off my bandana and ripped the duct tape off my mouth.

"Ouch!" Britt and I both said at the same time. After they ripped the duct tape off us, they left.

"Hey, we need some answers here!" Britt said. We were surrounded by several children. I saw a couple of people who looked like they were about seventeen, but they were the oldest.

"Mimi, are you okay?" Britt said.

"Yeah, I am fine. Next time we are kidnapped and put into a car, never talk again, okay?"

"I will try my hardest," Brittney said. I do not understand her sometimes. I think she just freaks out and cannot help but talk. I looked at everyone, trying to see if I knew anybody.

"Do you see anybody you know, Britt?" I asked.

"Yeah, actually, I think I do." She grabbed my hand and started to run to whoever she was looking for.

"Hey, Josh," Britt said to the guy. She tapped him on the shoulder. He turned around. Josh was really tall. I was surprised Brittney was able to reach his shoulder.

"Britt," he said. He did not seem to be happy to see her, while she had a big grin on her face. I am pretty sure he was scared.

"What is going on? We were basically dragged out of her house!" Britt said while pointing at me.

"Honestly, I don't know. I was dragged out of my friend's house too." He pointed to his friend. I did not even know anyone was there.

"Hi, I'm—," Britt interrupted Josh's friend.

"Nice to meet you. Anyway, does anybody understand what the heck is going on here because I do not understand at all and I am partially freaking out!" Britt screamed. In all the years I'd known her—since second grade—I'd never seen her act like this.

"Calm down, Britt. Try to be a little patient, and maybe you will get some answers. They have us here for a reason, and they will probably tell us what is going on."

"I'm with her," Josh said.

"So who exactly are you guys?" Josh's friend asked.

"I am Mimi, and this is Brittney. Who are you?" I asked as nicely as possible.

"My name is Chase Collins," he said. He had a pretty deep voice. He looked about fifteen or sixteen.

"Well, nice to meet you," Britt said with a fake smile. I knew it was fake. She was just trying to be patient like I told her.

"You know what I would like to know?" Chase asked. We all looked at him, waiting for him to get to the point. "Where are all the adults? I mean, if you notice, there are not any parents or adults except the people that brought us here." He was absolutely right. Why were there only kids here? It didn't make any sense. What did they do with all of these children's parents? Then I thought, *The parents must all be in the same area.* They had to do something. I didn't know what was going on. They probably didn't either.

"That makes a lot of sense, but the question is: how are they involved in this?" Josh said. I thought about it. My mind was completely blank. I had no idea what they had to do with this situation.

"Maybe they made some type of decision, or maybe they told our parents a lie and our parents agreed to let them take us. I really don't know," Britt said. I wondered why Britt involved herself in the conversation. Actually, the only reason she was here was because of me. If she hadn't come to my house, she would not be in this mess.

"Britt, you do know I am the only reason why you are here, right? If you weren't at my house, you would not be here. I think it has something to do with how much money our parents make, and your parents make enough," I told Britt. She knew it was true. I felt bad about it too. I didn't know what was going to happen to us in the next hour, but I knew it was not anything good. I had a bad feeling in the pit of my stomach, and usually that means nothing good.

"Mimi, it is not your fault. I came to your house on my own, and I was not supposed to be over there in the first place," Britt said calmly. She wasn't freaking out as much anymore.

We were all quiet. We all knew the rest of our lives were going to change. I was wondering why we were just standing here without any advisor. I felt someone tap me on the shoulder. It scared me so much I was afraid to turn around. Britt looked to see who was behind me and yelled.

"Ashley!" Britt said. I turned around, and there she was. I could tell she was happy.

"Hey! Oh my gosh! I have been so alone. I was walking to your house, Mimi, and someone just grabbed me and put me in their backseat. What is going on?" Ashley was scared. She had no one. At least Britt and

I had each other, and Josh and Chase had each other too.

"We don't know. We are trying to figure that out also. I think everybody is," Chase said. Ashley just looked up. I could tell she was trying to figure out who he was.

"I am Chase, by the way," he said again. Ashley just smiled.

"How long have you been here?" Ash asked.

"Not that long," Britt said. "You?"

"I just got here, and you were the first person I saw. I am really scared, Mimi! What is going to happen?"

"It is okay, Ash. We are going to find out. I think right now we just need to stick together."

I had to try to calm everyone down. That was basically my job—calm everyone down while I was freaking out on the inside. But I had no one to calm me down.

"Attention!" someone said into a microphone.

Everyone got quiet.

"Attention, children. You are all probably wondering why you're here. Well, Congress passed a law saying that parents who make less than $50,000 a year are not eligible to take care of their children. Therefore, their children will be taken to a live-in facility where they will attend classes early in the morning. Your advisor will explain once you get there. We decided to make it more fun for you children, so instead of driving there, you can walk like you are going camping. There is a trail specifically made for you kids. Depending on your behavior, you will either have to walk and set up a tent, or we will put you on a bus instead of walking to your destination. If you veer from the track, you will be severely punished. You're not able to ride on the bus more than three days in a row. This means most days you are walking. You are all going to be separated into groups with a maximum of twenty-five people each. Some groups will have less. Each group will follow different paths and trails but end up in the same place. It takes about a month to get to your final destination. Each group has two leaders." He named each group. After each group was called, they were given clothes and food and started walking on their private path. I did not listen until I heard my name.

Our leaders were Harold Jackson and David Skigh, the two guys who had brought Brittney and me to this awful place. "In this group, the following kids are Chase Collins, Henry Done, Ashley Herdkins, Jackson Bull, Perry Rhode, Kendall Pary, John Quary, Brittney Palms, Meredith Jones, Josh Brown, Andrew John, Alexander Wary, Liz Taylor, Emily Done, Jason Hurley, and Taylor Wright. You have the smallest group, so you will definitely be doing most of the walking. I promise, at the end of this trail you will be in a better place. Now go to your leaders over there."

"Thank goodness we are all in the same group," Britt said. We all started walking to our leaders. Once we got to them, they recognized Brittney.

"Nice to see you again, sir," Britt said sarcastically. By the looks on their faces, they were not glad to see her again.

"Not you ten-year-old again!" one of the guys said.

"We are not ten, thank you; we are fourteen. A pretty big difference, I might like to add." Britt seemed as though she loved to mess with them. I think this "trip to a better place" was going to make her day better, since she would get to mess with them.

"Well, my name is Harold Jackson, and this is David Skigh," said the guy who did not like Britt. "Here are your clothes and food for the day." Each of us got a backpack full of all the stuff we needed. The kids in our group were not that much older than us. Three people looked like they were about seventeen. Four kids looked like they were ten. I knew it had to be bad for the ten-year-old. They probably weren't happy. A lot of the kids were crying. They tried to suck it up. It was sad. I wondered what I would do if I had to leave the only thing I knew when I was ten. It would have been horrible.

"Now come on and start on our trail." They seemed kind of nice, but I knew that was soon going to change. I felt like they were putting on a show. I walked alongside Brittney and Ashley. Josh and Chase were right behind us.

"I do not think they are telling us the truth," Ashley whispered to Britt and me.

"Neither do I," Britt said. "But I think for right now, we should just play along. Soon we will find out what is going on."

I agreed with Britt. We just needed to keep our mouths closed until they gave us real answers. We had been walking for about ten minutes when my feet started to ache.

"Ow," I mumbled. I did not want anyone to know I was already tired. I noticed a little girl walking alone. She seemed to be exhausted. I walked over to her.

"Hey, little girl, what is your name?" She looked a little frightened.

"Taylor," she said with a half sob, half moan.

"Well, if you're tired, I will carry you," I said in the nicest way as possible.

"Thank you, but right now I am fine. I can do it," she said and walked away. When she walked away, it almost seemed as if she was trying to run away. If I were her, I would have said thank you and then hopped right onto the person's back.

"Oh, okay. Well, when you get tired, just tell me." I walked back to Ashley and Britt. She acted like I tried to kill her or something.

"What did you say to the girl?" Ash asked.

"I just asked her if she wanted me to carry her. Gosh, it's not like I was trying to slit her throat."

"Well, do you honestly believe she is going to say yes to a stranger, Mimi?" Ash said. She made a point, but if I were that little girl, I would say yes in a heartbeat.

"Umm … yes." I said. Ashley just rolled her eyes at me. We kept walking for what felt like hours. Why would they make us *walk* to a "better place"? Shouldn't we be in an airplane, or at least a car? It did not make any sense at all. I guess they just wanted it to seem like a camping trip for fun. Maybe it was the least they could do since they were taking us away from our families. The two leaders stopped.

Harold said, "This is our rest stop. Each rest stop is about ten minutes. We are close to our destination for the day. We will walk about two more hours until we get to where we are sleeping. So for right now, you can just eat some of your food." Harold looked like he was in a hurry. I guessed he really did not want to do this.

The rest stop was a large circle with a campfire in the middle and log benches to sit on. Trees surrounded us. I never really paid attention to how it looked. It was as if we were going hiking and we had to stay on a specific trail or something. I sat next to Ashley and Britt. I unzipped my backpack and realized there was no food in it.

"Sir, I have no food in my backpack."

They ignored me. I knew they heard me, but I believe they refused to care. A guy who looked about seventeen walked up to me. I wondered what he was going to do.

"Hi, I'm Alex." He smiled. I think he was trying to do the same thing I did with Taylor.

"Hey. I am Mimi. Nice to meet you," I said, trying to make sure he knew I was not afraid of him. He had his food in his hand a sandwich and two bags of Doritos. He handed a bag of Doritos to me.

"You can have some of my food if you want," he said. I did not understand why he was being so nice, but I could not accept his offer.

"No, I couldn't. It is your food. Thank you, though."

He didn't listen. He just put the bag of Doritos right beside me, smiled, and walked back to where he was sitting. I didn't understand why he was being so nice to me.

"Who was that?" Britt asked. *Do my friends ever pay attention?*

"His name is Alex, and he gave Mimi some of his food," Ashley said. *I guess they actually do.*

"Aw, someone has a crush on Mimi!" Britt said jokingly.

"Eww, he is way too old for her, and he was just being nice," Ash said to Britt.

"I was just kidding. Gosh, Ash, take a chill pill," Britt said. She rolled her eyes. Josh and Chase were coming our way. Josh sat next to Britt, and Chase set next to me.

"Who were you talking to, Mimi?" Josh asked. Seriously, it was not that crucial. I was talking to a boy for ten seconds; big deal. Apparently everyone was paying attention!

"He offered her some of his food," Britt said.

"Mimi, he is way too old for you, and you know it," Josh said. I could not believe it.

"First of all, he was being polite. Second of all, do I even know you? I don't think so. I am pretty sure I just met you today. Actually, I didn't even meet you. I just heard Britt over there saying your name. So why do you care?" I yelled. Everyone got quiet, including the little kids introducing themselves to each other. Everyone was looking at me.

"Sorry, Josh," I whispered.

"It's okay," he whispered back.

"Nothing to see here," Britt said. Everyone turned around and finished what they were doing.

"Goodness, Mimi. You didn't have to scream," Ash said.

"Honestly, I did not mean to. Sorry, Josh, I was … I don't know." He just smiled and said, "I understand." Chase looked at the bag of the Doritos.

"Aren't you going to eat those?" I completely forgot about them.

"It has been like seven minutes already. I will just eat them later," I said and put them in my backpack. I looked to where Alex was sitting all alone. He did not have anyone to talk to. Alex was really tall and very slim. He had brown wavy hair and hazel eyes. I must have been staring at him for a while because soon his head started to turn my direction. I turned away as fast as I could before he could see that I was ever looking at him in the first place. I turned back around, and he wasn't looking at me anymore. I continued to stare at him while he ate his sandwich. He seemed kind of depressed actually, as though a lot was on his mind. Eventually he turned back around, and I pretended like I was not looking at him to begin with again. I felt like it was going to last for ever. Then I turned around and he was laughing. I did not understand why, so I just kept my head down.

"Okay, the ten minutes are over. We are going to continue walking for another two hours, so come on." This time David was talking. I could not remember his last name. We all started walking. Britt and Ash kept looking at me mischievously.

"What?" I said.

"We saw you looking at him. It was funny because every single time he caught you looking at him, you would turn away," Ash said. I turned around and saw

Alex was walking alone. I walked over to him, knowing once again Ash and Britt were going to be watching me.

"Hey, Alex," I said. He smiled.

"You didn't eat the Doritos," he said.

"I wasn't that hungry. I promise I will eat them later," I said. "So how old are you?" I asked.

"Seventeen. You?" I was right. I am good at figuring out people's ages. He was pretty tall. I wondered why they made him come here in the first place. If they were taking us to this place that was supposed to be like a boarding school, he'd only be there for about four months.

"Fourteen," I said.

"That's cool." Being fourteen isn't that cool. I think he was just saying something.

"Why were you laughing at me?" I asked, even though I was pretty positive I knew the answer.

"You kept looking at me, and every time I would look up, you would turn away," he said.

"Well, it is kind of weird when you are looking at someone and they catch you looking at them." He laughed. "See my point?" I added.

"Yes, I completely understand," he said sarcastically.

"Fine then, I will leave," I said.

"Okay, then leave," he said in an uncaring voice. I did not want to. I was just assuming he was going to say "No, I will stop" or something like that, but his face seemed like he could care less.

"Well, fine. You can be depressed all by yourself," I said. I still was not walking away.

"Okay, bye," he said.

"Bye!" I said.

"You aren't moving," he said. I looked down at my feet. I was still walking right next to him. He realized I was not going to walk away.

"Sorry, Mimi. I will not laugh at you for the rest of the day," he said. I felt like he was still being sarcastic, but I could not really tell.

"Thank you," I said as I tripped and almost fell on the ground. I heard Britt and Ashley chuckle. They were watching me. Again! Really? Do they have anything else to do? I looked at Alex, and he was trying his hardest not to laugh.

"Go ahead," I said. He didn't. He just kept walking and didn't say anything. It was quiet for a while.

"All of your friends are watching you. Including that guy over there," he said. I turned around to see what guy he was talking about. It was Chase. Chase turned around right when I saw him too.

"That guy is not really my friend. I just met him today. But those girls are Britt and Ashley. I have known them since elementary school," I said.

"Oh." He waved at Britt and Ash. Ashley turned around, and Britt waved back. Then Ashley hit her and pushed her to turn around.

"They seem … cool," he said hesitantly. We kept walking. I just decided to ask him questions.

"So, why exactly are you here? I mean, did they like shove you in a car or what?" I asked.

"Well, my parents sort of let them. They just explained to them the new law Congress passed. They didn't care or do anything," he said. The tone of his voice didn't sound depressed, but I could tell by his eyes that he was. I would be too if my parents basically didn't care about me. "They were not my real parents. Thank goodness. I was adopted," he said. I did not want to ask him anything else about his life. I was scared to. It was kind of sad he was in a family that did not care about him; that was ready to get him out of the house. I wondered if my mom was fighting to get me back. I hoped she was. I knew she cared about me. I knew she would not just let me be taken, no matter what the government said.

"So how were you taken away from your home?" Alex asked.

"Well, basically, my mom wasn't home, and Britt just came to my house. Then we thought that Ashley was at the door, but it was really those two guys right there at my doorstep. They just threw us into the car," I said while pointing at everyone I mentioned.

"Oh, well that was nicer than how they took me. I really don't believe they are taking us to a 'better place,'" Alex said. It does not make any sense." He was right. I didn't believe it either.

"Right now, we should just play along. I think for the first couple of days they will be nice," I said.

"Yeah, until we get far enough that there is no turning back!" That made a lot of sense, but I really did not know. There was a possibility they were taking us to a better place.

"They could be taking us to a certain type of boarding school," I said.

"Yep, that is exactly what they are doing. Taking us to a boarding school and letting us walk there so we will not crash into a tree! Mimi, just think about it for a second. Why would they make us walk? They are trying to torture us!" He probably was right, but I still had to be the optimistic person.

"We do not know that for sure, so just play along for now," I whispered. I did not want anybody to hear us. I saw the little kids. They looked so tired. The little girl who had declined my offer to carry her walked up to me.

"My feet really hurt," she said, looking straight up at me with longing eyes. I guess that was her way of saying "Can you pick me up because I'm dying here?" She was so small. She could pass as seven, but I was pretty sure she was ten.

"Here you go," I said and put her on my back, but I think my backpack was uncomfortable for her. She did not bicker.

"We have five little kids in our group. We need to start taking care of them," I said to Alex. Alex rolled his eyes at me. Maybe he just didn't like kids.

"They seem fine to me right now." I looked up. All of them were out of breath, as though they were about to pass out. One boy literally looked like he was about to have an asthma attack.

"Yeah … right, Alex." He went to a little girl and mumbled something to her. Then he put her on his back and walked back to me.

"Are you happy?" he said.

"Ecstatic," I said sarcastically. I saw that a lot of the teenagers were picking up the little kids and putting them on their backs. People really do watch me. I saw Chase put a little boy on his back. I think the girl who was on mine was already asleep. We kept walking. It felt like five hours had already passed. I did not have a watch on, so I didn't know.

"They are almost asleep," Alex said, annoyed. He must have not had any adopted younger siblings to take care of. I had no siblings, and even I wanted to take care of them. He seemed like he did not care.

"I am thirsty," Alex said. I had a bottle of water in my backpack, but Taylor was on it.

"Here, hold her for a second." I took her off my back and put her in Alex's arms. I opened my backpack and found a bottle of water. Then I zipped my back pack up and gave my water bottle to him while he gave me back Taylor.

"Thank you," he said.

"See, now we are even!" I said.

"A bag of Doritos for a bottle of water. I think the bag of Doritos are more valuable."

"No way. Water is something you need. Doritos are just a piece of junk," I said.

"Oh, so now you are saying that what I gave you is a piece of junk? Wow, that really hurt," he said.

"That's not what I meant. It came out wrong," I said. He just laughed.

"I was just kidding, Mimi. Do you know how to take a joke?" he said.

"Yes, I do, and you said you would not laugh at me."

"Oh, I was not laughing at you. I was laughing with you," he said. I was confused because I was not laughing at all.

"But I was not laughing," I said. He just rolled his eyes at me. I didn't understand. I just decided to drop it. It was getting late. It had to be about five or six, and I thought we were almost done.

"Wow, it is getting dark," I said.

"Yep, usually the time changes and it becomes night when it gets dark. It is an every-day process." He laughed. He said it really slowly as if he were mocking me. I hit him, but he kept laughing. He was so mean to me. It was really unnecessary for him to be so offensive. Sometimes it will take me a while to understand things, but that doesn't mean I am slow.

"We are close to our rest stop. This is where we are going to be sleeping. There are two big showers. One is for boys, and the other is for the girls. You have everything you need right in front of you," Harold said. He and the other guy walked away. I took Taylor off me. She was awake. Then I walked to Britt and Ash.

"Hey," I said. They just looked at me. "Come on; I want to take a shower right now," Britt said.

I got my clothes from my backpack and took them with me. The shower was one big shower divided by curtains. It was outdoors too. It was a little disgusting, but I could deal with it. I took a shower, washed my face, and brushed my teeth. They gave me a pair of gray sweatpants and a white t-shirt that practically swallowed me. Britt and Ashley were already done.

"You take too long," Britt said.

"So what happened between you and that Alex guy?" Ash said.

"Nothing. We were just talking. He was walking all alone, so I just went over there and talked to him." Britt did not believe me.

"He is too old for you, Mimi," Britt said for the second time.

"We do not like each other like that, and I barely even know him. He is actually kind of mean," I said.

"Britt, you should not just jump to conclusions," Ash said.

All the guys were trying to build a fire. Surprisingly, they got it burning pretty quickly. Somebody set the tents up. There were five tents that could hold three or four people each.

"This one is ours," Britt said. There was nothing special about it. They were the exact same. The one she picked was the second to the right. Right beside ours, Josh and Chase pitched theirs. I put my stuff in my tent and walked to where the fire was. I sat down by myself while everyone was picking tents. I felt someone breathing behind me. I turned around, and it was Chase.

"Hey," I said.

"Hey." He sat down right next to me. "That walk was tough," he said.

"Yeah, I know. I feel kind of bad for all the younger kids," I said.

"Me too. I saw you help that little girl out," he said. I must be an interesting person because Britt and

Ashley were always watching me, and apparently, he was too.

"I saw you too." I looked up at him. He looked so distressed. Sweat was dripping from his nose. I didn't think he had ever walked that long of a distance. I wondered if I was sweating as much as he was, but I had just taken a shower. Maybe it was water from the shower.

"I would have never thought about it if you did not do it first. It is pretty weird for them because they have to talk to random strangers like they have known them their whole life. Then again, so do we." It was completely true. I was talking to him like he was my best friend, and I had only known him for five hours. I never thought about it like that. It got quiet.

"Mimi!" I turned around. It was Alex.

"I am not talking to you!" I said.

"Why?"

"Because you are so mean to me! Thank you very much. I am not slow."

"I never said you were."

"You acted like it."

"Okay, fine. Don't talk to me," he said it in his uncaring voice. Alex was so rude.

"Fine," I said. "I will not talk to you at all for the rest of this ... whatever it is."

"Then why are you still talking to me?" he whispered, smiling.

"Ugh." I walked away to my tent. Ash and Britt were still in there.

"Where did you go?" Britt asked.

"I was by the fire," I said. Britt whispered something to Ashley. Ashley just told her to shut up, but she was laughing too. I guessed it had something to do with Alex. I realized I was really hungry because I had not eaten at all.

"What are we going to eat?" I asked.

"The food they gave us," Britt said. I had none.

"You can have some of mine, Mimi," Ash said.

"Thank you, but I will just eat my Doritos." I got my bag of Doritos and finally ate them. I was pretty sure Alex would leave me alone about the Doritos.

"Britt, you had something to tell us. What was it?" Ash said.

"It does not matter anymore." Britt was lying. She was stuttering, and when she does that, it is obvious she is lying. She started looking around the tent as if she was trying to change the subject. "Just tell us," I commanded.

"Well, I have a boyfriend." It was not that big of a deal. She usually had one, but they lasted about a week.

"Who?" Ash asked.

"Josh." We were quiet. They didn't even talk, but I was pretty surprised it was him. She always had a boyfriend, but Josh hadn't really talked to her today.

"Aw, but why did you not talk to him at all this afternoon?" Ash asked.

"Because once Mimi went to go talk to that Alex guy I did not want to leave you alone. He also did not want anybody to know yet." That was surprising. It was not really that big of a shocker, but Josh just seemed like her friend.

"Well, I think we should go out to the fire. I think Josh is there," Britt said. We got out of the tent and walked to the campfire. Every kid was there, but the leaders weren't. I wondered what they did. I saw Alex at the campfire. He was talking to a guy who looked about his age. I guess he finally made some friends. I saw Chase and decided to sit by him.

"Hey, sorry I left. That Alex guy is so mean," I said. He just looked at me.

"If he is so mean, then why were you walking with him all day?"

"That is actually a really good question, but I've only talked to him once, and that was today. I guess I'm just meeting new people," I said. Chase looked away. I didn't think he wanted to talk to me anymore. I looked over at where Alex was. He was just talking to his friend. They were laughing about something. I did not want to think about him right now anyway. I was supposed to be mad at him. I really was not that mad. I was just messing with him the same way he was messing with me all day.

"Why are you looking at him?" Chase asked.

"Well, we were just talking about him, so I was wondering where he was." I completely made that up. Chase didn't look at me again.

"So what do you think is going to happen to us?" I asked Chase. He still did not seem like he was in the mood for conversation.

"I do not know." He shrugged. He seemed really mad, and I guess he had a right to be. I had just completely ditched him because of Alex, but why did he care so much?

"Look, I am sorry that I ditched you, but will you please forgive me?" I whined and gave him the puppy dog face. I did it horribly, so it would be funny if it actually worked. He would not look at me. I just got right in front of him so he would not turn around. He laughed.

"I forgive you." He said it so properly. It was silent for a few seconds. "I don't get it."

"Get what?" I asked.

"Everyone is so calm. We have been rushed out of our houses, these guys tell us we are going to a new facility, and we act like we are fine with it. It makes no sense." He was right. We are all acting like we were in a camp, when really we all had no idea what it was. We didn't know what was going to happen in the next month. We didn't even know what was going to happen the next day.

"I think for right now everyone is trying not to worry. I think they would rather believe and have hope that everything is okay than freak out to find out exactly what is going on," I said.

"I guess," he said.

"Well, how exactly did the officers who came to take us break into your house?"

"It all started when Josh came to my house. We were basically just having fun until we heard someone ring the doorbell. They did not tell us anything; they just shoved us into their car. They were huge too," he remembered.

"Wow. At least they said something to us. They just shoved you into the car." I started looking for Britt. She was sitting next to Josh, of course, but I did not see Ashley. I searched for her. She was sitting next to this little girl, talking to her. Then I looked at Chase. He was searching for someone, but I did not know who. Then he just looked at me and smiled.

"Mimi!" said a familiar voice. I turned around.

"What, Alex?" I said with an attitude. I laughed so he would know I was just kidding. He sat down next to me.

"You haven't introduced me to your friend." He smiled. I think he was trying to annoy me. First impressions are important, and my first impression of Alex was an annoying guy who had no life but to annoy me.

"I am Chase," Chase said. He seemed a little irritated. He wasn't the only one.

"Hi, Chase. I am Alex." He seemed so friendly.

"Can I talk to Mimi for a second?" Alex asked Chase. Chase just nodded his head. We got up and walked closer to where the tents are.

"I see you are making friends," I said, laughing at Alex. Finally he was not laughing at me.

"Do not worry about me, Meredith. That guy is getting mad at you." *What the heck is he talking about? How does he know my name?*

"Who?"

"Chase! Honestly, I do believe you are slow. I can tell he likes you."

"He does not know me," I said.

"He is trying to get to! Go back over there." I did not feel like it because I was tired. Besides, I didn't want a boyfriend right now. All of us had just gotten taken away from our homes. We didn't know where we were going, and right then I would rather try to figure that out than worry about my social life.

"No, I am going to bed. Tell him I went to sleep, okay? I promise you I will walk with him in the morning, okay?" I told Alex. He walked away. I walked to my tent and fell asleep. I was so tired. I was glad the day was over, but I was scared for the next one.

# THREE

"Wake up!" Britt hit me with a pillow.

"It is time to get up, so help us make our tent and get our food, clothes, and whatever else we need!" She seemed cranky. I guessed she did not get enough sleep last night.

We folded our tent up, and Britt threw it right next to the leader's foot; but he did not notice. We brushed our teeth, washed our faces, and got our clothes, food, and everything. There was a small station on a table that had our name and what we were going to get. Under my name, there were two turkey sandwiches, three bags of chips, two t-shirts, and a pair of jeans. There were also two pairs of underwear and a bra. Thank goodness! I went into the shower and changed into a different t-shirt. After that, I put all my stuff into my backpack and was ready to go on the walk. Chase was ready too. I was kind of scared to go over there. I felt like he was mad at me. He walked over to me. I turned around to make sure he was walking toward me and not anyone else. I did not see anybody else. He was right next to me.

"Hey." He smiled what seemed like a friendly smile.

"Hey. Are you ready for this long walk?" I tried not to talk about yesterday.

"Yep. You?"

"Not really." I was getting really nervous. I could not even talk to him. I guess it was because I was confused. I mean, wasn't he mad at me? I was not going to bring it up.

"I understand. I am not ready either. The only thing I am ready for is this thing to be over." I was pretty sure a lot of people wanted that.

I saw Alex. He was trying to signal me something. I think he was trying to say "Talk to him."

"I think we are about to start walking," Chase said. He was pointing to something behind me. I turned around and saw our two leaders.

"Come on. We are starting our destination for today. We will get there in about ten hours," Harold said. He started walking. Everyone followed him.

"So how old are you?" I asked Chase.

"I turn fifteen in eighteen days. How old are you?" he said.

"I am fourteen. Happy early birthday." That was going to suck. He was going to celebrate his birthday walking. He just laughed and said thanks.

"Why aren't you walking with Alex today?" Chase asked. He always was wondering about Alex.

"Because I just don't feel like it right now."

"Oh." It got quiet. I felt like I had to make conversation with Chase to get him to talk. Was he like really shy? Most of the time he did talk, but right now he wasn't.

"So," I said. There was nothing else to say.

"What do you like to do? Your favorite hobbies?" Chase asked me. I really did not have one.

"I don't know. I guess I am a pretty boring person. What about you?"

"Well, I like to skateboard. It is pretty fun. I am not that good, but I like it." *Chase* seemed like a skateboarding type of name. I always wanted to learn how to skateboard, but I would rather not break my bones.

"Wow, that is cool. Have you ever broken a bone or even sprained an ankle?" I asked. He nodded his head and pointed at his arm. I had never broken any bone in my body, and I really did not intend to.

"Do you like anyone?" Chase asked me. It reminded me of what Alex had told me last night. I didn't think he liked me. He still didn't know anything about me.

"No. Do you?" He got quiet.

"Not really."

"Did you know Josh and Britt are going out?" I asked him. He nodded his head.

"Told me yesterday while we were walking." I turned around and saw Britt and Josh walking together. Ash was walking with the little girl she talked to by the fire last night. I saw Alex walking with his friend. He looked at me.

"Turn around," he mouthed. I did so. Why did he want something to happen between Chase and me so badly?

We kept walking. The day went by fast. We had already had a rest stop. Everyone was tired already. I know I was. My feet ached. I was still walking with Chase. I looked up at him. I realized how pretty his eyes were. I could not even understand the color. I kept walking while looking at his eyes. He was looking at something else, so he did not notice. I felt my foot get stuck in a little hole. I could not move. I felt like I was about to fall over, but someone grabbed me out of it and pulled my foot out of the ditch.

"Are you okay?" Chase asked.

"I'm fine. Thanks." I knew Alex and Britt were laughing at me. Chase didn't laugh though. I turned around, and Britt was laughing. So was Josh. Ash was not paying attention. Alex was laughing hysterically. I turned back around. I was so tired of Alex being so rude. Didn't he have a life? If he did he could find something better to do than make fun of me.

"Everyone is laughing," I whispered.

"It doesn't matter. They just have no lives." He smiled. That was exactly what I was thinking.

"I met you yesterday, and I saw you trip." Gosh, didn't everybody?

"Yeah, I am pretty clumsy," I said. It was sadly true. He just laughed.

"Hey! That isn't funny," I said.

"Sorry." He was quiet.

"I was just kidding. I partially do not care."

"Partially?" he said as if he didn't understand.

"Yeah, well, I don't really care, but if you come with a smart comeback, then I will get annoyed, like somebody I know." He knew who I was talking about and started laughing.

"He needs to show you some respect!" Chase said. He was being sarcastic.

"Exactly. Finally someone understands." I smiled. I looked down or straight ahead when I talked to him.

"Attention. We have another rest stop," Harold said. He just rolled his eyes then sat down. I was glad the leaders were not saying much to us.

I got my backpack to see if it had any water in it. I realized that I never got any.

"I don't have any water," I said. I do not think anyone heard me. Alex was walking by.

"Hey, Alex, do you have any water?" He looked at me.

"Didn't I already give you a bag of chips?"

"Well, do you?" I asked.

"Yes."

"May I have some?" I said, getting irritated.

"I will think about it." He turned around and left. I sat right next to Chase again. He was sitting next to Ash, Britt, and Josh.

"Hey, I don't have any water," I said to Britt.

"Neither do I. Josh gave me his because he got two bottles of water," Britt said. Goodness, why do I always have to ask my friends for stuff? They never give me anything, but Alex gave me food yesterday. They didn't. That is called tough love.

Someone tapped me on the shoulder.

"Here you go." I turned around. Alex had a water bottle in his hand.

"Aw, thanks. You actually are a nice person," I said, smiling. I was going to see if he was going to take it personally. He just glared at me and walked away. I turned around. Ash and Britt were looking at me.

"What?" They didn't say anything.

"Anyway, Josh has a plan to run away," Britt said. She gazed at him and smiled.

"I think at night we should run off the track and try to find our way," Josh said. That was stupid plan. I think everyone thought about that and then thought of the consequences.

"No offense, but think about it. They said that if anybody got off the trail, then someone will get punished. That probably means that there is a way they can tell if someone gets off the trail. Also, what about everybody else? We cannot just leave all these little kids by themselves," I said.

"She is right," Ash said.

"Let's say that they have something like an alarm system if you cross the trail. If they did, I don't think they will keep it during the whole trail. They probably have it for the first couple of miles and then close to the end of the trail they assume no one would try to reach cross it. Maybe they deactivate it and think it is useless," Chase said. That was a possibility.

"But how far?" I asked. "I mean, if it is too far, it would be stupid just to turn back."

"Then we would have to take that risk," Chase said.

"Okay, how about this. We discuss it tonight by the fire. Everyone except for the kids. They do not need to know. We do not want to freak them out," I suggested. It was settled. We had to get back on the trail and finish the rest of the day. I told Alex, and he told some of his friends about the plan. After I told Alex, I kept walking with Chase. We did not really talk about much. Taylor asked me to carry her again, so I did. Soon, the day was over. I took a shower, and the boys set up all the tents and created a fire. The leaders did not do anything. They had two tents. They were farther away from our little area. I put my backpack in my tent. Ash and Britt were in there.

"You are finally talking to someone your own age," Britt said.

"Shut up, Brittney."

"What about you, Ashley? You were talking to that little girl."

"Yeah, she is adorable. She just told me that she is going to miss her mom, but she is glad she is going to a better place. They think this is actually something good, Mimi. We all know that there is something fishy about this. We are not going to frighten them," Ash said.

"Yeah, I know. That is why I do not want them in the meeting today. Let's go take them to bed right now." Britt and Ash agreed. We got out of our tent. All the little girls were done taking showers. I saw Taylor.

"Hey, Taylor, it is time to go to bed, okay? You have a big day tomorrow," I said in the nicest way possible.

"Okay, Mimi; let me go get my friend Emily."

I let her. I walked them both to their tent. There was already another girl in her tent, the girl Ash was always with.

"Here you go, Taylor and Emily. Good night," I said with a smile. I closed their tent up. I saw Ashley.

"Hey, did you get the boys?" I asked her.

"No, Britt did." Britt was running to us.

"I got the boys into their tent. Now we can go to the fire and discuss this 'better place thing,' whatever we want to call it." She looked as if someone had just run over her multiple times.

"Gosh, it was tiring putting those boys in their tent," she said. That explained why she was so out of breath. We walked over to the fire. Everybody else was already seated. Ash and Britt were right next to me. No one said anything. I just decided to start the meeting.

"Hi, I am Mimi, and I wanted to talk about this whole 'better place thing.'" Everyone was quiet, waiting for me to keep on talking. "Well, we all know that they are not telling us the truth. So what do you guys think we need to do?" I asked.

"We have a plan. Remember when we got here? They told us if we got off the trail we would be severely punished. Maybe there is a tracking device that tells them that someone has gotten off the trail. Close to the end of the trail they probably deactivate it," Britt said.

"If they do have something like a tracking device, can't we just take it from them?" said someone in the crowd. That actually sounded a lot easier.

"You couldn't just do that. They probably have a tracking device with them, but the government could track us down. It would make more sense if they just deactivate it at the end of the trail instead of us taking it away from them," Alex said.

"But we do not even know for sure if they do have an alarm system on the trail," someone said. That was true. We were just guessing.

"I don't think they would make it that easy to run away. I am pretty sure they know we don't believe them," the guy that was talking to Alex all the time said.

"How about this? We have a little test." Alex had a strange grin on his face while tapping his fingertips together, almost as if this was an evil plan. "Henry and I will pretend we were fighting. Then he will push me off the trail and I will fall." I guessed Henry was his friend since he pointed to him when he said his name.

"That actually is a pretty good idea. So it is settled. We will do that tomorrow?" I asked everyone. They nodded their heads. Everyone got up to go to the tents.

"Wait. We will have this meeting again tomorrow. Make sure all the kids are in their tents, asleep! Also, we need to talk about what we are going to do with the kids. They believe this 'better place' thing. They do not know any better," Ashley said. Everyone went to the tents. I was walking and then Alex was right behind me.

"What?" I said.

"I was just going to say that was a good idea. That there are alarms around the whole trail," he said. I did not understand why he was complimenting me. Most of the time he made fun of me.

"Thanks. That was a good plan for you and Henry to do," I said, trying to be nice.

"Why, thank you very much. See, you're nice too," he said, smiling.

"Shut up! I am always nice," I said. He laughed and walked to his tent. *I knew it. All he does is think he is super cool. I don't understand why he loves torturing me, though.* He was walking back to his tent. I noticed that when he walked, he put his shoulders back and almost moved them side to side with each step he took.

I walked back to my tent. Ash and Britt were trying to go to sleep.

"What took you so long?" Britt asked sleepily.

"I was talking to Alex," I said. She and Ash raised their heads in surprise.

"Why are you always talking to him?" Britt asked.

"He is always talking to me. I guess he is kind of my … friend." It took a long time to get word *friend* out. But even though he was annoying sometimes, I still loved talking to him.

"What about you and Josh?" I asked Britt.

"What about him?" she said. I guess she did not want to talk about it.

"Nothing. Goodnight," I said. I lay down and went to sleep.

# FOUR

The next day seemed the same as yesterday. Today was the big day. Alex and Henry were going to act out the fight. He told me not to worry because he had a good plan. I didn't. Everyone kept asking me about it, though. I'd tell them, "Alex and Henry have it under control." I really did not know if that was true. Alex did not seem like that type of person—someone you could depend on to do something that involved many people's lives.

"We are about to do it. Tell everyone," Henry whispered to me. I told everyone that they were about to do it.

"Shut up! I'm tired of you!" Alex said and pushed Henry. I could tell that he was trying not to laugh.

"Do not push me!" Henry said. Henry pushed him so hard he fell rolling off the trail. I looked right at the leaders. One of them had something beeping in his pocket. He took it out of his pocket. He looked at it and turned around.

"What is going on? Who got off the trail?" Harold said. His face was bright red with anger.

Alex was walking back onto the trail. Harold looked straight at him. He walked over to him and grabbed the neck of his shirt.

"Tryin'a run away?" Harold said. There was something different with Harold. Usually he tried to be nice, but now he seemed almost evil. He said it in such a low voice. Everyone was frightened. I knew I was.

"I pushed him, sir," Henry said. He was stuttering. I guess I would be too if I was in his position.

"Trying to protect him, eh?" Harold said with a big, evil grin on his face. Whatever the punishment was when a person crossed the trail, he was ready to give it to Alex. His face was completely blank. I guess he didn't want to show any fear.

"Leave them alone. That kid said he just pushed him," the other leader said. Harold turned around, still holding Alex. Alex was pretty tall, but Harold was a giant. He looked about six foot ten! He wasn't slim like Alex, either. Harold had a body like a linebacker.

"These kids know what they're doing! They are trying to run away!" he yelled. He was really mad. I really didn't understand. All he did was roll over the trail.

"So you admit there is something to run away from," Britt said. If Britt wasn't careful, her mouth would get her in trouble someday—like now! Harold walked up to her while still dragging Alex by his shirt. She looked terrified. Her face froze. She didn't move at all. For once, her mouth was closed shut.

"I remember you. You're that girl with the smart mouth. Now listen, young lady; I don't want to hurt a girl. So I would suggest you watch your mouth," he said. He walked back in front where the other leader was and kept Alex beside him for the rest of the day. I kind of felt bad for Alex. Although he wasn't dragging him by his collar anymore, it was still kind of scary. Now I knew that they weren't nice people. We finally saw their real colors today. Except David. He probably really did not want to do this—whatever they were doing—but had to. I was walking with Chase. We did not really talk. No one did after that whole thing. Henry walked up to me.

"What do you think he is going to do to Alex?" Henry whispered to me. I actually never thought about them doing anything to him. I thought the dragging by the shirt was punishment enough.

"I don't think they're going to do anything," I said. I mean, why would they? They knew it was just an accident. At least the other leader did. Harold just wanted someone to punish. I felt weird calling Harold, Harold. I mean, it would sound better calling him *Mr.* Harold. But he did not deserve that respect. They apparently believed we deserved nothing, those of us whose parents made less than $50,000 a year. Now they were taking us who knows where to rot in the dirt, just like their filthy hearts.

"Well, he said that he was going to be brutally punished." I never remembered the *brutally* part, but he did. I tried not to think about it. Alex was a tough guy, at least I thought he was. I did not think they were going to do anything to him. I really did not want to think about it. It gave me a bad feeling in my stomach. I was worried about what they were going to do to him. Maybe they were not going to do anything. I kept walking. I could not stop thinking about it. I had horrible thoughts. What if they tortured him in ways that you could not imagine, like starving him, tying him up, and beating him almost to death?

"Mimi, he will be okay," Chase said. Was it obvious I was thinking about him? Could people tell?

"I know he will be okay. What makes you think that?" I said, basically lying. I did not know if he would be okay. I needed to stop worrying so much. Right now he was fine. They weren't torturing him.

"Well, you are crying," Chase said. I touched my face. It was completely wet. My shirt was soaked. How can a person cry and not know it?

I wiped my tears and tried to think of a sunset at the beach. The weather was hot. There was a slight breeze. The sounds of the waves were beautiful, but the waves were huge. That was a good thing. I was standing in the water. It was not too cold and not too hot. I could see sea creatures. The sea creatures were around me. Seashells were along the coast. Jellyfish were in the water. They did not harm me, though. They swam away from me. I tripped and was about to fall into the water. Except when I fell, I did not feel water. I felt dirt.

"Mimi, are you okay?" Chase said. He helped me back up. He actually kind of just picked me back up. I nodded yes. He must be really strong. Chase was not a buff person, but his arm muscles were huge. Usually he caught me before I fell. That time, he just let me fall flat on my face. He must have been wondering what I was doing. I did not even know. I think I was imagining and walking with my eyes closed. I do not understand how I always fall. Thank goodness no one was looking at me. Usually everyone is, but I think they were too busy wondering what was going to happen to Alex too.

"We have a break. It will be extended to twenty minutes today," David said. We all sat down, except Alex. I did not see where he went. Actually, I did not see the leaders either. After they announced our break, I just sat down, turned around, and they were nowhere to be found. I went to Henry.

"Where did he go?" I asked Henry.

"I don't know. Maybe they are going to do something to him." Henry seemed a little worried too. I think he was trying not to show it.

"Well, the plan did not go as expected, but I did notice the leader pull something out of his pocket. That showed him someone was off the trail," I told Henry.

"Do they not pay attention to us? They should have been able to tell that we were fighting by all the noise we were making." I never thought about that. That meant that they would not be paying attention to us a lot. It would be easier to leave.

"Yeah, but my point is that we were right. They do have a tracking device. All we have to do is find out if it is ever deactivated and when it is," I said.

"Okay, we will have a meeting tonight, right? We will talk about it," Henry said. I walked away and sat next to Britt and Ash.

"What happened to Alex?" Ash asked me. Apparently, everyone was worried about him.

"I do not know," I said. "But I think that they extended our break for a reason. If you notice, our leaders aren't here and neither is Alex." Britt and Ash looked around. They did not see them either.

"Oh my gosh … what are they going to do to him?" Ash said. She was freaking out like I was. Ash was a caring person. She had never even talked to the guy, and she was worrying almost as much as I was.

"Aw, Mimi, are you okay? I know he was your friend," Britt said. A lot of people had asked me that today.

"Yeah, I am fine," I lied. Britt knew when I was lying. Somehow, she could tell. But she did not say anything for once. She knew not to. I think she was going to decide to listen to Harold and try not to say anything. Ash gave me a big hug.

"I don't think they are going to keep him for that long. I think he will be back," Ash said. She was right. It was not like they were going to kill him. *Oh gosh, why did I have to think that? Don't cry! Don't cry! Forget it. Think of clouds in the sky. One of the shapes is a balloon. The balloon has something written on it: "Calm down."*

"Mimi, are you sure you're okay?" Ash said. I must have been thinking too hard.

"Umm…yeah, I am perfectly fine. You don't need to worry about me," I said. But really I was freaking out. My mind was not functioning right. *I just need to calm down,* I thought. *Breathe in. Breathe out. Breathe in, breathe out.* That calmed me down a little. That was as calm as I was going to get. I opened my eyes.

Ash and Britt were looking at me like I was insane. I really didn't blame them. I just ignored them. I got out my food. It was a salad. Finally, there was something different for lunch than a sandwich. I realized they did not give us that much food. David came back.

"Okay, we are going to finish our destination for the day without Harold," David said. I wondered why they said it like that. "Our destination for the day" sounded so weird. No one asked where Harold was.

I was pretty sure they knew that he was with Alex. I tried not to think about it. I just kept walking, ready for the day to be over. Soon we were done for the day. The little girl, Taylor, did not ask me to pick her up today. I guessed she realized she had to get stronger because we still had a long way to go.

I took a shower. When I finished, I put the little girls in their tents. I was hoping that Henry or someone would put the little boys in their tent. I went to the campfire for the meeting, which I was not going to start today. I didn't want to start it today. My whole body was aching with pain, and not because of the walking.

"Hey, guys. Well, our plan did not go as we planned, so we can't really worry about that right now. Mimi said she saw something blinking in Harold's pocket after Alex crossed the trail. Maybe we were right. They do have something detecting when we cross the trail. Now we just have to find out if they ever deactivate it," Britt said.

"Maybe if we try to get the thing that was beeping in his pocket, it will tell us, someone said. It could work, but it would be really risky.

"I think that is too risky, but then again, it is the only way to find out. In order to do this, we have to come up with a really good plan. Not like the one that happened today," I said. Everyone got quiet.

"We have to be more careful. That Harold guy is insane. Maybe when Alex comes back he will have more information," Ash said.

"What if he doesn't?" a girl said.

"Let's not worry about that right now. Let's just think when he comes back we will have information, okay," I said.

"Well, we will talk when we get enough information. Remember, we need to talk about the kids. We need to take care of them. See you in our next meeting," Ash said. Everyone went to their tents. Ash and Britt seemed like they didn't want to sleep.

"Are you going to be okay?" Ash asked me.

"Am I okay about what?" I knew what she was talking about; I just did not want to talk about it. I knew I was going to anyway.

"You know, Alex and stuff," Britt said.

"I am pretty sure he is okay. We do not know where he is, and we don't have to think the worst. He is probably just in a different area or something," I said, raising my voice above a whisper. I really did not want to talk about if he was okay or not. I knew if I thought the worst I would start crying and worry about him. I didn't understand why I cared so much. I had known him for three days. It really was not that crucial. He was a friend, but maybe it was the fact that he could have been my best friend. If he didn't come back, then I wouldn't be able to get as close to him as I could have. That didn't sound so bad. He was mean to me anyway. I laughed in my head.

"Mimi, it is okay to be worried and wonder where he is. We are your best friends, and we're here for you," Ash said. Britt nodded.

"I am not worried. I barely even knew him, and it has only been a day. I am pretty sure he will be back tomorrow. You guys can just chill," I lied. I knew he wasn't going to be back tomorrow. I was pretty sure everyone did. It sucked that this happened.

"You don't have to put on an act. We have told each other everything. You can trust us," Britt said.

"Honestly, I am worried. It just is weird because I barely knew him and he was a good friend. I mean, I knew him for like three days, but it was like I had known him for three years. It is kind of weird because, besides you two, he is the only reason why I made it this far. I really liked him as a friend, and we could have been closer as friends, but now he is gone. Gosh, why am I talking like he is dead?" In the middle of that, I started crying. I knew I was going to end up crying anyway. Ash just hugged me and kept saying it would be okay.

"He will be back to help us get out of this mess, Mimi. We all know it. Maybe not tomorrow, but he will be back," Britt said. Their words weren't necessarily helpful, but they could not really do anything.

We finally went to sleep. I cried myself to sleep that night. I had never really done that. It surprised me that I would do this over a guy I had known for three days.

The next day, he still wasn't there. He wasn't there the day after that either. It felt like a week had passed and he still was not there. I cried so much because there was a possibility he was dead. No one had seen him for days. Both leaders were there, though. Harold had come back around two days ago. He seemed ready to get someone in trouble. Everyone was more alert. Every day when we walked, I tried not to think about Alex. But it was hard.

"Hey," Chase said.

"Hey." I tried to smile.

"Are you going to the meeting today?" he asked.

"I guess. Why?" He must have asked because I hadn't been going to them since Alex wasn't around.

"Well, you haven't gone and are missing a lot."

"Britt and Ash tell me everything that goes on. Don't worry," I said. I started walking faster, but he kept my pace.

"Why haven't you been going?" It seemed as though he wanted to talk about Alex.

"I have been tired." That was true, but it wasn't the only reason.

"We hardly ever talk about the incident." I knew he was talking about Alex. He said it like Alex was a thing.

"That is not the reason, and I really do not want to talk about it." I tried to say it in the most respectful way without making it seem like I was getting irritated with him, even though I was.

"Oh, okay. So how are you?" he said. I decided just to make conversation.

"I am okay I guess. You?"

"Pretty scared." I understood why.

"Yeah, I understand. We have no idea where we're going," I said. He looked at me.

"That's not just it. We know it is something bad. What if they just make us walk around for a couple of days to mess with us? They basically told us that the government made a law so that parents who don't make enough money are not eligible to raise their children. They are taking us to our own special school, or whatever, and none of us are freaking out. What about our parents? We do not know what they are doing, and I am pretty sure most of them are worried sick. He made a point. The government passed a law that said that parents who made less than $50,000 a year couldn't take care of their children. I guess that made sense for people with lots of children, but with a single child, it didn't.

"That doesn't make any sense. I think $50,000 is enough money for a single child, but maybe not ten children. There is something fishy about that. I do not believe that is the complete truth," I said.

"Well, yeah, all along we knew it was fishy, but we were thinking it didn't make any sense for all the wrong reasons. Now let's try to put ourselves in the government's place." I thought about it. Nothing seemed to click. It didn't seem right. What were they really doing?

"Maybe we should not be asking these sorts of questions. We should keep tagging along," I said.

"But that is not going to get us anywhere," he said. It was true.

"Remember, we said that the device around the trail probably deactivates somewhere. Honestly, it probably doesn't deactivate till we are closer to the end. They might believe it is useless to keep it because there is no point in running away anymore."

"Why would they deactivate it anyway?" he said. That was a good question.

"Maybe they did not have enough money to waste on the last couple of days."

"But if you're going to spend some of your money and have a little left, you might as well spend the rest." He was right again, but exactly where were we heading?

"It is probably not our territory. Maybe soon we will reach a different country and they did not want people to be wondering why they would need a tracking device around the trail."

"They could just make up an excuse, like if the children get lost and if it was close to the end of the trail. Then wouldn't they be suspicious where they were taking them?" That made sense. They probably wouldn't take us out of the country.

"Where exactly are we? I mean, we have been walking for a while. And I am pretty sure there isn't this much free land left."

"That doesn't seem right either."

"Yeah, a lot of this doesn't seem right," I said. I was now confused more than ever. Once we got to our final destination, I was ready for the meeting. I decided I did not have a right to lead it today, so I just sat down. I was the first one there, and then people started showing up. Chase sat by me.

"Hey. Are you glad you're here tonight?" he said.

"Yup." I was ready to talk about whatever was going to be brought up. I was just hoping no one would say anything about Alex since I was here. Ash and Britt were finally there.

"Hey, everyone," Britt said.

"Well, today we have decided to talk about Alex. We have no idea where he is, but when he comes back, he will have a lot of information about what is going on," Ash said. *Great, when I decide to come back, they talk about him. I should have known they were going to talk about him, especially since I was here.*

"What exactly is there to talk about? I mean, he is gone. What can we say?" a girl from the crowd said. It was the same girl who talked last time. She flipped her long, thick brown hair and raised her voice as if she had an attitude.

"That may be true, but we need to talk about how we are not going to let it happen again. There are so many things we do not understand, like where we are going, where are we in the first place, and why they are doing this?" I said.

"That is why we need to escape now," the same girl said.

"That will be acting stupid. Why would we escape from something we don't know? I do not think we should just think fast. I think we need to think smart," I said.

The girl finally was quiet.

"You're right, but we don't have that much time to find out," Henry said.

"They said this trip is about a month. It has been about two weeks. I think we have enough time to start getting busy and come up with smart plans," I said. I really had no suggestions.

"Well, what do you think is a smart plan?" Britt asked me. I thought about it.

"I really don't know," I said. I tried to think of something. "Remember the detector in Harold's pocket? It probably explains where we are and everything. We have to somehow get it from him," I said.

"Yeah, but how?" Chase said. *Everyone always comes up with good questions to go against my plans.*

"We have to come up with a plan, and a good plan that we all discuss."

"We will plan it tomorrow. It is getting late, and we need our rest for tomorrow. Also, tomorrow, everyone will take one of the younger children and try to find out what they think about this whole situation. Okay, well, goodnight," Ash said. Everyone went to their tents. I was kind of happy about the meeting. Maybe we were actually getting somewhere.

"Hey," Ash said to me. I turned around.

"I'm happy you came today." We were getting in the tent.

"Yeah, me too," I said.

"We rarely even bring up Alex," Britt said.

"I wonder where he is," Ash said. It had been a week since he was taken. No one had seen him or heard from him. I was hoping he was still alive. I didn't think they would kill him.

"I hope he is ... alive," I said. I didn't want to say it because I was pretty sure he wasn't. None of us were sure if he was alive or not. We were walking on a trail with two leaders who would probably try to harm us. I really did not even want to think about it. I just decided to lay my head down and sleep.

# FIVE

When I woke up, I got my backpack and was ready to begin to walk. It seemed as though Henry had something urgent to tell me because he rushed toward me when we began walking.

"You are going to be excited," he said with a big grin on his face. I wondered why he looked like he was going to break his face.

"Why?" I said.

"Because Alex came to my tent last night after the meeting. He told me to tell you he was fine. But he has a lot of information." I was in shock. I think I started to grin like he was. I was going to scream with joy, but I decided not to because then everyone would look at me like I was weird.

"Wait; why isn't he here?" I asked him.

"Well, apparently, where they have him staying is like a quarter of a mile away from here. He snuck out and just headed west. He overheard the people who took him explaining everything while he was pretending to go to sleep. He is going to be back in a couple of days, though."

"Well, what did they do to him?" I asked urgently. I needed to know.

"I don't really know. He didn't want to talk about it, but he had this huge bruise on his arm. I don't think it was his only one either," he said. They were abusing him. I kind of figured that. I was just happy he was alive, but he could have come to my tent instead of Henry's. It didn't matter. He was alive and was going to be back in a couple of days.

"Well, what did you find out?"

"Well, apparently, Congress passed a law that any parent who makes less than $50,000 is not eligible to take care of their children and they will be immediately taken away from them. We already know that, but most people who actually care are wondering where the children are going. That is a problem for Congress because they are not planning on doing anything to help us. But something bad happened. Someone who was a part of the Senate told a family member what actually is going on and what they are planning to do with us. Then the word got out, and Congress is trying to cover it up," Henry said. He did not tell me exactly what they were going to do to us. He seemed like he was hoping I would not ask. I did not think it was going to be a good thing either.

"Henry, what are they going to do to us?" He looked at me, seemingly terrified of the words to come out of his mouth.

"Well, the truth is that the world is getting too populated. They do not have enough space for everyone. So ..." He did not finish. He did not need to. I already knew.

"So what, Henry?" I said, afraid of what he was going to say. All the blood had stopped flowing through my body. I was frozen. I couldn't even move my fingers. I could barely hear properly.

"So they are going to annihilate anyone who makes less than $50,000 a year. They are going to kill us, Mimi. They just have us walking around to make it seem like they are getting something done and for us to believe that we are going to a boarding school or whatever." My heart stopped. I wanted to pass out. I couldn't see where I was going. It was worse than I ever thought. They were going to kill us. They were trying to get rid of us to make more room in the United States. Well, couldn't they just ship us to another country? They had probably already tried and failed. Probably all the other countries were overpopulated also. Then I thought about it.

"If they are so overpopulated, then why can't they just build more houses here? I mean, it seems like a lot of clear land where we are walking," I said.

"I don't know, but I know they need places to build crops and produce our food. Since we are getting over-populated, there are not as many places they can produce and farm anymore. Food is becoming scarce."

"What about our parents?" I asked.

"No, they have them in jail, but they will kill them if they try to fight back." The government was cruel. It made sense, though. I think they could have found a better way to deal with this than killing people. We weren't necessarily poor. We just weren't multimillion-aires or anything near that. But I believed that they could find a better way to stop from getting overpopulated and the food from getting scarce. "Does anybody know about it?" I asked.

"No, I am planning on announcing it tonight at the meeting," he said. I did not even know what to think. It seemed so unrealistic. Why would anyone even consider killing thousands of people to stop the world from getting overpopulated? At least people were fighting back. At least people were going to start protesting. That is why the government did not tell the truth, because they knew that people were going to go against it. Maybe even countries would get involved.

We got to the campsite at noon, and I was tired and furious and scared all at the same time. I was ready for the meeting. I wondered how everyone was going to take it. I was not really scared of them killing us. I had a feeling God was not going to let them. I had a feeling that we would get out of this mess soon and alive.

"Hey, I am Mimi, as some of you guys know. Henry found out some news about what the government is really planning on doing to us, and Henry is going to tell you," I said. My heart was pounding extremely fast. I was kind of nervous of what was going to happen. Henry stood up ready to talk.

"Well, Alex came to my tent last night. He is staying a quarter of a mile away from us and has found out some news. He said that Congress passed a law that anyone who makes less than $50,000 is not eligible to take care of their children, as we know, but we all had a feeling that wasn't true. Apparently, so do all the citizens that do make more than that. They do not believe it either. Well, someone leaked that Congress actually thinks that the country is getting too over-populated and the food is getting scarce because there is barely that much free land for crops and stuff. They were actually planning on killing every child whose parents make less than 50,000 dollars a year, and some people are protesting against it," Henry said. Everyone sat down and was quiet. Ash was crying, whispering, "We're going to die." Britt was crying too. Then I remembered Britt wasn't even supposed to be here. Her parents weren't rich, but they made enough money.

The only reason she was here was because of me. This was my entire fault. I would hate to be in her position and I am the one who brought her here. I started to cry. I walked over to Britt.

"I am so sorry, Britt, for getting you into this. If it weren't for me, you would be at home, not worrying." She looked at me.

"It was my choice, and if I were at home, I would be crying my eyes out because I would think two of my best friends were dead. This is worth it. If we die, at least I die with you. If we die, I have no regrets that I came to your house, but hopefully we will escape," she said with tears in her eyes. I could feel my heart pounding in my chest. If I cried any more, then I probably wouldn't be able to breathe. We were all hugging each other. It was sad to *think* that these were the last moments of our lives. It was even more terrifying to *know* they were. I still had hope—hope that we weren't going to die, hope that we were going to get out of this. I got up and made an announcement.

"We have to escape from this. I think we still need to get the deactivator from Harold. We have to find a way to distract him. These are our lives, and not just ours, but thousands of others. We need to escape and then try to make a difference," I said. People nodded their heads.

"It's true. I don't know about you guys, but my mom raised me to not go down without a fight. We need to find a way to get out of here, and I think the detector is our only hope," said the same girl who spoke up yesterday. Everyone was quiet.

"So are we all in?" I asked. Everyone nodded yes.

"I don't think we need to tell the kids. They probably do not need to know because then they would be scared to death," I said. Everyone agreed. I walked over to the girl who had agreed with me.

"Hey, what's your name?"

"Kendall," she said somewhat impatiently.

"Well, you made some good points yesterday and today."

"So did you." She looked about my age. Maybe she was a little older. I only thought that because she was taller.

"How old are you?" I asked.

"Fifteen. You?"

"I am fourteen." She seemed shocked.

"You seem older. You always make good points when you're at the meetings. Well, I am going to sleep, so I'll see you tomorrow."

"Bye."

She kind of seemed nice but acted like she was in hurry to go to her tent. I could not blame her. I was tired too. I went to my tent. Ash and Britt were already in there.

"What do you think is going to happen to us, Mimi?" Ash asked. Her face was still puffy from crying.

"I have a feeling that we are going to survive," I said. I truly did.

"Why would Congress want to do this? They should be ashamed for even considering such a cruel thing. This is not fair at all," Britt said. She knew she did not need to be here. I felt so bad about it. I did not want to cause her any pain. "I am sorry," I said.

"It is not your fault at all. Honestly, I am glad I am here with you two. If I wasn't, I don't even know what I would do," she said, looking me straight in the eyes. I think she was serious.

"We should go to sleep," Ash said.

"Good night," Britt and I said at the same time.

I could not go to sleep. I could hear Britt snoring. I just thought about life, about what was going to happen in the next few weeks. I did not want to wonder if we were going to live or die. I hoped my mom was okay. I doubted she was okay, but I hoped she was alive. I think she was hoping the same for me. I wondered where my mom was. Hopefully she was in a safe place. Suddenly I heard someone at the tent, and I could see someone's shadow. It scared me. I prayed it wasn't a leader.

"Mimi, it is Alex." My heart skipped a beat. I unzipped the tent and stepped out. I think I had the biggest grin on my face. I ran to him and hugged him. I didn't even say anything. It felt like minutes went by, but I did not care. I hadn't seen him in a week.

"Ow," he said after about four minutes. I let go.

"Sorry." I took a step back and examined him. He looked horrible. He didn't look like he had taken a shower since he left. He looked skinnier than he was when he left. He was trying to smile, but I think he was in pain.

"What did they do to you?"

"You don't want to know." He looked serious. I couldn't see the bruise on his arm because he was wearing a jacket. I did not see any bruises on his face, but it was dark.

"I do want to know," I said. He shrugged.

"They tortured me, Mimi. In ways your mind can't even handle. At first, I was taken to this little shed somewhere here. It was Harold and two other guys. He was telling them how I tried to run away. So they all took turns hitting me. They did that every day. They also wouldn't give me food. I ate every other day and barely got any water. When they said we would be severely punished, they meant it. But the good in this is that at night when they thought I was asleep, they would talk about everything. That's how I found out so much. Apparently, we are just walking in circles. This is a lot that's about eight hundred acres. Each trail is about a quarter of a mile apart. Ours is the farthest east. All we have to do is go that way and try not to go pass the other alarm, but I will explain tomorrow. They tried to kill me, though. They almost did, but they decided not to. They wanted to be nice, even though they are going to kill us all later. They are just stupid. I can't say what I want to, but still. I was tied up to a chair, but then at night they untied me and threw me on the floor to sleep." I felt bad for him for all the stuff that he had gone through. I really missed him. It was hard for me not to hug him.

"I'm sorry. At least we will find away to get out of here," I said.

"Well, how has it been without me? Have you been talking to that Chase guy?" He raised his eyebrows. I just laughed.

"Nothing special has happened except what we found out today after you went to visit Henry, and Chase is just my friend. I don't want to be any more than that, although he does have really pretty eyes."

"Now, I am sad that you don't like him. You would have made adorable babies." He made a sad face. I ignored him.

"Shut up! Now I remember how annoying you were." I rolled my eyes at him. He was still laughing.

"If I am so annoying, then why did you cry when I left?" He was making a sad face and then started laughing.

"I was not! I would never cry over you, and besides, why did you not come to my tent last night instead of Henry's?" I asked him. I lied about crying, and I was not really mad at him about it, but I wanted to know.

"Oh, you did not cry at all over me? That is not what Henry said. I did not come because I doubted you would be awake and Henry is a really good friend of mine. He is kind of like a brother to me. You know what I mean. Plus, we share the same tent." I realized I was not a really good friend to him. I realized that he did not care about me the way I did for him.

"Yeah, I understand. He is a good friend to you," I said.

"Yeah. Well, honestly, did you cry?" he asked.

"I cried a little bit because you could have been dead and a lot of people thought you were and…" I really didn't want to tell him I cared about him.

"And…" He was going to try to make me say it.

"I don't know."

"Yes, you do!" He seemed happy to torture me.

"Why do you care?"

"Because it's fun."

"Fun doing what?"

"Messing with you." I should have known he was going to say that.

"Why do you like messing with me? Can't you find someone else?" I was kind of mad that he just talked to me to mess with me. Was I just a joke to him? I wondered if he honestly thought of me as a friend or just a person who entertained him when he was bored.

"Nope." He smiled. He did not realize that I was about to cry. Gosh, I hated crying. I just didn't like caring for him because he didn't care about me at all. He just liked to mess with me as though I was an item. To him, I was like the nerd all the popular people loved to pick at. I had cried way too many times over him. My eyelids were getting heavy. If I blinked, a tear was going to go down. I pretended to yawn and then blinked before he could notice that I was crying.

"You still didn't tell me."

"You don't deserve to know." I didn't look at him.

"Are you mad at me?"

"Yes!" I still didn't look at him.

"Whatever."

"Okay, fine. I'll just go back into my tent and let you go back to wherever you are supposed to be." I was about to unzip my tent.

"Mimi."

"What?" I wasn't going to let him see my face.

"Are you okay?"

"I'm fine." Now I could hear it in my voice. I was about to cry.

"I'm sorry." It was the first time he said sorry to me and actually meant it.

"Do you even know why you are saying sorry?"

"I know that I hurt your feelings, but I really don't know what I did." I finally looked at him but didn't say anything.

"Why are you crying?" He looked at me weird. That moment, I realized something. I realized I liked him. I didn't just care about him as a friend. I thought the reason why I didn't tell him I cried was because I cared about him. That wasn't true. But I didn't want him to know it. I didn't want to feel it, but sadly, I did. I would try to tell him like a friend.

"You are my friend, or at least that's how I think of you. You never take me seriously. I mean, it's okay when we are just joking around, but when I am serious, you still joke around. Do you even truly consider me a friend?"

"I don't think of you as a joke. You are like a little sister to me. That's why I treat you the way I do." He probably thought that I was being a little overdramatic, but he didn't know how I really felt. It didn't matter because all he did was think of me as a sister. I wished I only thought of him as a brother, but I didn't.

"I understand. I'm sorry for getting so mad to the point where I cried when it wasn't really a big deal."

"Well, you still didn't tell me." I was hoping he was going to give it a rest.

"I was going to say you're my friend," I said. I kind of lied, but technically he was my friend.

"Why was that a big deal?"

"Because you were going to get big headed and mess with me as usual." That was actually true. Knowing him, he would.

"Well, see you tomorrow. I am back for good hopefully."

"Bye." I didn't hug him. I just went to my tent.

"Hey, what was that noise?" Britt said. She was half-asleep.

"Nothing, just go back to bed." She did. I laid down. I did not want to like him the way I did. It wasn't fair. This should be the last thing on my mind. All of us were about to die, and I was thinking about him. I barely even knew him. Why did I care so much? *I don't like him at all.* Usually when I lie to myself, it works. This was not working.

# SIX

I was so tired. I didn't feel like walking at all. I got up anyway and was ready to begin the journey of the day. Our leaders seemed as though they had something to tell us.

"Today we are not walking. Today we have a bus ride. The bus will show up in about five minutes." I was so happy that we were going on the bus. I think everyone was. I looked around, and everyone seemed happy, but it faded quickly. We all remembered how they were going to kill us. Well, how they were planning to kill us. I wanted to escape. Now we didn't know anything really. Maybe Alex had some more information that he did not want to talk about. I wondered how he was able to cross the trail when he snuck to come see Henry and me.

I looked for Alex. He was wearing a t-shirt, so I could see the bruise on his arm. It looked like someone had pushed him onto the ground in the same spot fifty times. I did not see any other major bruises. It seemed as though everything else was just scratches and scrapes. I turned around. Britt and Ash were right in front of me.

"I'm glad we're getting on the bus," Britt said. She did not show a smile on her face. I think it was because they were going to kill us anyway.

"Yeah, me too."

"Hey, there's Alex. Wow, he looks like they slaughtered him and then brought him back to life. You should go talk to him," Ash said.

"No, thank you. I'd rather not," I said. They both looked confused.

"Mimi, you have been basically depressed for a whole week since he was gone. You don't want to talk to him at all?" Britt had a point, but she didn't know I had talked to him last night.

"I already did, and I don't want to talk to him again."

"When?" Britt asked. I told them the whole story about how he came to my tent and started messing with me, how I got mad because I realized that I cared about him more than he did for me, and how I did not want him to know I liked him. They were quiet.

"I knew you liked him," Britt said.

"I was hoping you wouldn't," Ash said.

"It really doesn't matter. He only looks at me as a little sister." I turned around to find him. He was laughing about something with Henry. How could he laugh at a time like this? I guess he felt he should embrace the good times while he could. Ash shook me back around.

"If you don't want him to know, then stop staring at him," Ash said. The bus was arriving.

"The bus is here," Harold said. It was just a yellow school bus. Nothing special. We all got on. I decided to sit in the back—not the last seat, but close to it. Henry and Alex sat in the last seat. Josh and Chase sat right across from them. Ash decided to sit in the front with the little kids to keep them company. Britt sat by me. We were in front all of the noisy boys. I was pretty sure Britt wanted to sit by Josh "If you want to sit by Josh, you can."

"He is already sitting next to Chase."

"Make Chase move," I said. She nodded her head. She went to Josh and asked him if he wanted to sit with her. He said of course. Chase moved and then sat by me. I did not want to sit by him right now. I wanted to talk to Alex.

"Hey," Chase said.

"Hey."

"You seem tired."

"I am. I think I am going to go to sleep."

"Okay," he said. I actually fell asleep. When I woke up, it still looked the same, except I wasn't sitting with Chase anymore. I was sitting with Alex. Even though I did want to talk to him, I didn't want to. I pretended

I was still asleep. I put my hand on the window and let my head hit my arm. It was the most uncomfortable way to sleep, but I pretended anyway. I think Alex soon found out I was faking.

"Mimi." He shook me.

"What?"

"Are you awake?"

"Yes." I put my head up and opened my eyes. "How long was I asleep?" I asked.

"About an hour."

"What happened to Chase?"

"He is sitting with Henry."

"So why are you sitting with me?"

"There was nowhere else to sit." I looked around me. There was an empty seat right across from me.

"There's a seat right there."

"Do you want me to move?" I really didn't.

"I don't care." He stayed in the same spot.

"Are you still mad at me?" I wasn't really mad at him. I was just mad.

"No, why?"

"You're acting weird."

I couldn't really breathe at all. *What if he knows I like him? Crap! There is no way! It's not obvious at all.* "How so?" I was surprised I was able to say something. I really did not want it to be obvious that I liked him.

"You're just not ... " I wondered what he was going to say.

"Not what?" *I need to calm down.*

"You." He acted like he knew me so well. Well, no one knows me except me.

"And exactly how do you know who I am? You have only known me for about two weeks, and one of those weeks you were gone." I was finally calm again.

"Well, you're not acting how you did when I first met you."

"Maybe because I am tired."

"Do you want to go back to sleep?"

"No, I am fine." He was acting like a mother.

"Why do you care so much?" I asked him.

"Why do you think?" How was I supposed to know? That's why I asked the question.

"I don't know."

"I already told you, you're like a sister to me." I guess that meant that he cared about me, but if he did, he could just say it. Then again, I wouldn't say it either. I didn't want to.

"Do you think we are going to die?"

"No, I think we can come up with a plan to escape."

"But after we escape, where do we go?"

"I don't know. We have to be able to stick together, and we have to move fast; somehow get out of their eight hundred acres of land."

"What all do you know?"

"Well, I know that they have an alarm around the trail and also their property of land. The only time they deactivate the trail is at night, but we won't be able to get past the land until the day they kill us. They deactivate it then. They also have detectors on our backpacks. When we escape, we can't bring them."

"So the only time we can escape is right before they try to kill us?" I asked.

"That I know of. We could get Harold's detector thing to see if there is any other way, but that's the only way I know of," he said. We would have to wait until the last day.

"We will tell everyone tonight at the meeting, and they will decide if we will stick to what you know or find out a way to get Harold's detector."

"Okay. Deal!"

"Deal." I high-fived him. I decided not to even think of liking him. It was the last thing that mattered right now. We had to find a way to get out of here alive. That was my goal.

"So what did you and Chase talk about?" Gosh, I should have known he was going to bring him up.

"Nothing. I went to sleep right when he came over here." He was obsessed with that guy for some reason.

"Oh ... well, you should have talked to him."

"Why! Whenever we talk it's just like we have to try to make a conversation. It's different with other friends."

"Like who?" I believed he wanted me to say him. This was why he liked messing with me; I'm an easy target.

"My friends, I mean he is my friend and all, but he isn't a person I can just talk to about anything that comes up."

"Well, make him that person."

"I can't. It's a natural thing." He laughed.

"It's a natural thing?" It is, though. It's not as if a person can just talk about anything to anybody.

"It's true!" He was still laughing.

"Well, why don't you go talk to that girl over there?" I pointed to Kendall.

"Who? Kendall?" he said.

"You know her?"

"Yeah, she's cool." *Oh, crap. He likes her.*

"Well, go talk to her," I said.

"No."

I already knew why. I could see it in his eyes that he liked her.

"Why?"

"She—I don't know."

"Aw, you like her." I felt like I was going to throw up, but if he liked her then I was happy for him…I guess.

"No, I don't." He was getting nervous. *I can't believe he likes her! Goodness!*

"That's adorable. Go talk to her." *Shut up! What am I doing?*

"Are you sure?" He was dead serious.

"Yes."

He walked over to her, and they started talking. I couldn't tell what they were talking about, but she was laughing. So was he. I couldn't believe this. He liked Kendall. Kendall, of all people. She was cool I guess, but random. I looked for Britt. She was laughing about something with Josh.

"Britt! Come here!"

"What!" she said. I felt like I was messing up her and Josh's alone time.

"Come here! Sorry, Josh, I just have to tell her something." Josh looked a little mad. Britt got up and sat by me.

"What?"

"Look." I pointed at Alex and Kendall. She looked.

"So…"

"So…he likes her. He just started getting nervous when I mentioned her, and then I told him to sit by her. Alex likes Kendall!"

"Oh, wow."

"Yeah."

"Maybe he thinks of her more as a girlfriend because they are closer to the same age." She was not helping at all.

"She is only fifteen."

"Yeah, but she turns sixteen in like a week." That reminded me of Chase's birthday.

"How do you know?"

"We talk every once in a while. I think she kind of likes him. She wasn't like you, crying and all that crap when he left, but she was sad."

"Yeah, I guess it is for the best."

"I'm sorry." She gave me a hug and went back to Josh. She wasn't really that mad. She was probably happy because he was too old for me. I looked at Chase.

"Chase, come here." He did as I said.

"What?"

"Is today your birthday?"

"Yeah, how did you know?" *I have a mind of gold.*

"I remember you told me. Happy Birthday!" I had to say it. He was happy I remembered.

"Thanks, you're the only one who has said it. Not even Josh over there." He pointed to Britt and Josh.

"I am guessing he wants his alone time with Britt." I laughed.

"How was your nap?" He sounded like Alex. It was as if they changed places.

"It was great. Thank you."

"What did you and Alex talk about?" *Wow, those two guys are alike in so many ways. Goodness, they are obsessed with each other.*

"Nothing, he was just being a jerk, as usual." I looked at him and Kendall laughing and talking.

"Aw, are you sad?" He laughed.

"Alex is always a jerk to me. You're acting like him right now."

"Sorry."

"It's okay. I was just kidding." He was acting like him, but not the jerk part.

"Oh."

"So are you ready to escape?"

"Yeah! I think everybody is."

"That's probably true."

"Apparently, we are walking on eight hundred acres of land. We're basically just walking in circles, and at night, they deactivate the alarm on the trail, but there is another one around this lot. The day they deactivate it is the day they kill us."

"If they have so much land and the world is getting too overpopulated, then why don't they use this land?" Chase asked.

"Because after they kill us, they are going to use this land for crops, houses, and other stuff."

"Why don't they just kill us already?"

"Congress wants it to seem like they are taking care of us. They want all the citizens to believe them, even though most people already know it's a lie. That probably means they're going to try to kill us sooner rather than later."

"Oh. This is still stupid."

"I know."

"I feel like we're in the Holocaust or something." He made a good point. It did feel like that. They were basically trying to exterminate us, but not because of our color or religion. This time it was because of our money, or lack thereof.

"It's discrimination. They are discriminating against how much money we make. They assume that since our parents make very little money, then we won't either."

"They believe that our lives matter the least." It was completely true. It wasn't fair at all, and it didn't make any sense. They needed to listen to everyone else before they started a war. *Like there isn't enough going on in the Middle East.*

"I think we will be able to run away. They kind of make it easy. I think they make it so easy because they believe that we're not educated enough to understand what's going on or to believe them."

"They believe we're stupid and we have never heard of anything called common sense!" I hated this. The government was going a little overboard with this.

"If you think about it, millions of people are going to die. Most people in America make less than $50,000 a year," I said. It was sad. It was sad that all the little children under ten years old were just going to be killed. Why would someone do that? Why would someone even consider taking a child's life? Why would someone consider taking anyone's life! This was so stupid!

"Well, I'm going to sit with Henry."

I saw Alex walking to sit next to me. That was probably why Chase moved.

"So how were you and Kendall?"

"She's cool." He didn't look so happy.

"You don't look ecstatic. Usually people do when they find their love!" I laughed.

"She's cool as a friend. Kind of like how you feel with Chase."

"Aw." I made a puppy dog face. Now I understood why he loved messing with people—it's fun. He rolled his eyes at me.

"So what about you and Chase?" He wanted to start torturing me again. I had my fun while it lasted.

"Nothing, we talked about this whole mess. A lot of people are going to die. Most people in America make less than $50,000 a year."

"But not all of them are parents. They are only killing children, remember?"

"A lot of them have multiple children, so therefore millions of people are going to die when they get done with this."

"Whatever."

"How can you say 'whatever' when a lot of people are going to die. Even if you are that selfish, you should know you're probably going to die too." He got mad.

"I'm not selfish. I really just don't want to talk about it!" I had never seen him get so mad. I didn't even say anything. I wanted to say sorry, but the words wouldn't come out. I just looked out the window. All I saw were trees. I was a little happy that he didn't like Kendall. It made my day, or maybe he didn't want to tell me. I really didn't know because they were laughing a lot. Now he was mad at me.

"Did you tell him what I told you?" he asked.

"If I say yes, will you be mad at me?"

"No."

"Then yes."

"Oh." He still seemed like he was in a bad mood.

"What's wrong?"

"Nothing, I just don't like talking about this stuff, people dying. It's what everyone thinks about." I remembered his parents died. He probably thought I forgot, which I had, until now.

"Oh." I tried to think of something that would get him to stop thinking about it.

"So are you ready to get off this bus?"

"Psh, no. Tomorrow we will have to walk again. I don't think I am ready for that." I forgot that he was basically bruised everywhere.

"I would carry you, but it'd look kind of weird." He laughed.

"I doubt you would be able to pick me up."

"Have you seen how skinny you are now?"

"I'm still taller than you."

"Doesn't go a long way."

"Sorry, but you're not going to be able to pick me up." He honestly believed that. I believed I could. He was skinnier than I was.

"That's what you think."

"We are so weird." I said.

"I know." I kind of liked it that way, our relationship as friends. It was fun to just talk about the most random stuff ever.

"Why are you looking like that?" he asked. I think I had a huge smile on my face.

"Like what?"

"Like you're so happy you are going to explode."

"I am just a happy person!" I smiled.

"Yeah, most of the time you're rolling your eyes at me and yelling." Now that I thought about it, that was actually true. That was basically all I ever did. That was his fault, though.

"I am not!"

"Well you don't really yell, but you do roll your eyes every ten seconds."

"Maybe because you are always making fun of me."

"It is a part of our friendship; I make fun of you, and you get mad and roll your eyes." I rolled my eyes. He laughed. I really needed to stop.

"You are so annoying." I tried my hardest not to roll my eyes.

"And you complain about everything."

"No I don't! I never complain." He started laughing again.

"Yes, you do! A lot. If I am just messing with you, you will get mad. Then I won't pay you any attention, and you will start talking to me again."

"That is true, but it proves my point. You mess with me a lot. That's the only reason why I complain."

"So it's my fault."

"Yep!" I smiled to make sure he knew that I was kidding. He laughed.

"You do smile a lot."

"Thank you."

"And you are so glad to be a happy person."

"Well, I wouldn't want to be sad all the time!" I remembered when I met him. He was so depressed, and right now he wasn't. Part of the reason why I was so happy was because I was trying to make him happy and not all grumpy like he was.

"I'm hungry," Alex said.

"I'm pretty sure you are." He got out his backpack. There was a sandwich as usual, but no bag of Doritos or anything. I guess they were still punishing him. I got out my backpack, and I had a bag of Doritos. I gave them to Alex. "Here you go."

"Now I owe you." He smiled and took them. I wasn't hungry at all. He didn't say anything while he was eating. He ate like a hungry animal, which made sense because they only let him eat twice a day.

"Sorry," Alex said while he was biting into a sandwich.

"About what?"

"You have to watch me eat like a pig."

"I don't have to; I can turn my head." He finished chewing.

"You know what, Mimi? You're a good person." I guess since he was surrounded by people who tortured him for pleasure, he forgot how it was for a person to be generous.

"It's not that big of a deal. Remember when we met, you gave me a bag of your chips. I think *you're* the nice person." It took him five minutes to finish his sandwich and eat half the bag of Doritos.

"In a weird way, I am happy they passed that law because I most likely would have never met you," I blurted out. It seemed awkward after I said that, and I don't like awkward moments. "Or anybody else here that I didn't know. They all seem like really cool people." I hoped that worked.

"Yeah, they are. I'm glad I got to meet the people I met." *Gosh, he didn't mention me, but technically I am one of the people he met. I am just going to shut my mind off now. If I say anything, I will soon get embarrassed because*

*I know he does not like me like that.* He finally finished his Doritos.

"Do we get bathroom breaks?" someone yelled.

"No," Harold said firmly.

"That sucks," Alex said. He started laughing. I think he enjoyed other people's pain. He certainly enjoyed making me mad. I suddenly got tired. I yawned and laid my head on the window again. It was very uncomfortable, but it was the only way. I would be asleep soon anyway. Suddenly I drifted to sleep. Someone was shaking me.

"Wake up!" someone yelled at me. I opened my eyes. It was Ash.

"Come on; get up!" I got up and off the bus. Apparently, we were at the campsite. I didn't see Alex. He probably ditched me while I was sleeping. I went to go take a shower and put my stuff in my tent. I walked out to the campfire. I sat alone. I saw Kendall right across from me. I walked over to her.

"Hey."

"Hey."

"Today we have even more information. Alex is going to tell us."

"Alex doesn't like talking about stuff like that," she said. She acted as if she knew him really well. I didn't think I would like this girl anymore.

"He doesn't really care; he just doesn't like it when you talk about people dying."

"Well, technically this and people dying are in the same concept." I felt like we were getting in an argument about Alex.

"I guess you could say that." I tried not to talk about it.

"Do you like him?" she asked me.

"Ew, no. He's like a big brother to me," I lied.

"Oh."

"Do you like him?"

"No, he's just my friend." She looked like she was telling the truth, or she was just a really good liar.

"Oh." I couldn't believe we were actually talking about Alex. I wished he wasn't special to me. I walked away from her. A lot of people showed up. Alex stood up as if to start the meeting.

"Okay, as you know, the government passed a law and blah, blah, blah. When I was gone, they said that we were just on a lot of eight hundred acres. Each trail is not that far apart. It makes it easier to escape. At night, they deactivate the alarm, but they still have one around the whole area. The only day they deactivate it is the day they kill us. They also have detectors on our backpacks that show where we are. Now we can try to escape the day they kill us, or find a way to get the detector or deactivator from Harold."

"I think we should just go with what he knows. It is too risky to try to get that device from Harold." A lot of people nodded.

"But what if they were just messing with him when he overheard them talking? They could have said that assuming we were going to try and run away. It could be a trap," Josh said.

"Okay, but how are we going to get it?" I asked.

"We would have to get the device at night so we will have enough time to realize how to use it," Henry said.

"Well, we have to watch where they go at night. We all make up our tents, but we never pay attention to where he goes or the other leader," I said.

"Do they use the same showers as you?" Kendall asked.

"No, I think there showers are farther down," Alex said.

"Tomorrow someone should go follow Harold and someone else should try to keep the other leader company."

"I'll do it," Chase volunteered.

"How about you and someone else keep David company? Then me and someone who knows how to work a deactivator will try and get it from Harold while he is taking a shower," I said.

"I'll go with you," Henry and Alex both said.

"Okay."

"This is really risky. If you get caught, you will get in so much trouble."

"Kendall, they're trying to kill us anyway," the guy that had to go to the bathroom on the bus said.

"Shut up, Jackson."

"This is really risky, but we have to take risks in order to get out of here," Ash said. They got quiet. I hoped everyone understood the plan.

"Let me go over the plan. Now, after we get to our campsite tomorrow, Chase is going to try to distract the other leader while Henry, Alex, and I follow Harold." Everyone nodded.

"Why do we need to distract the other leader and leave him with us?" Jackson asked.

"So when we take the deactivator away from Harold, he won't be around to see it."

"Oh, okay, gotcha."

"So is it a deal?" Everyone nodded yes. It was late, so we all went to sleep. I wasn't that tired since I had slept most of the bus ride. I was ready for the next day to come.

# SEVEN

It was the day of the plan. I was anxious, especially since the last plan didn't go so well. I was ready for it to happen. I didn't want to wait any longer, but I would have to wait ten hours. I really didn't think Alex should have volunteered. I didn't think we would get caught; I just thought he would have been scared after the last plan and wouldn't want to volunteer.

Today we didn't have a bus. We had to walk. I didn't want to walk. I was tired of walking every day. It was boring and hurt my feet. I think everyone felt that way. I looked around while we were walking. I was walking alone. Everyone seemed to be happy. I think they felt like these were the last days of their lives and they should make the best of them. I didn't believe we were going to die anytime soon. I hoped that the world would realize what the government was doing and try to go against it. I had faith. It was not right to take people from their homes and take their lives away in the process. I didn't believe it was the government's choice. I thought there was a better way. They could do a lot with the land we were walking on.

"Are you ready for today?" Henry asked. He was right behind me, walking with Alex.

"I guess, but I don't want anything to happen like last time."

"Don't worry, Mimi. Nothing will happen. I think this is a better plan, but we have to be super quiet when we walk. I just hope to get it over with soon."

"Who actually thinks they know how to use the thing?" I knew I didn't know how to use the deactivator.

"I do. I usually am good with electronics," Henry said.

"We are going to take turns following him. When I say that, I mean that I will walk five steps, then you will walk five steps. Do you get it?"

"Yeah, we get it," Alex said. Alex actually rolled his eyes at me. I ignored it.

"We have to be careful, especially since Alex is coming again. Last time they tortured him. This time they might kill him," Henry said.

"They're planning on killing all of us; it really isn't a big deal," Alex said.

"Well, my life is," Henry said. Henry had a point. They're going to kill us all, but we didn't have to let them kill us now.

"Well, we'll just make sure we are really careful," I said.

"I am just ready for this day to be over so we can get to do it," Alex said.

I was ready for the day to be over too. I was scared of what was going to happen, though. I did not want Alex to get in trouble again. Henry was right. If he got caught this time, he would die. We had to be careful, very careful. I didn't want him getting hurt. I definitely didn't want him to die. I was scared for him. I was not going to cry again. *Think of something different. My mom. I wonder what she is doing right now. I wonder if she is thinking of me as well. I miss her.* A lot of people missed their parents. I saw Taylor. She was with two other girls whose names I forgot. I walked up to her.

"Hey, Taylor." I smiled.

"Hey, Mimi. These are my friends Emily and Perry," she said. They all looked adorable. Perry was the tallest. She was the little girl Ash used to always walk with. She wasn't near my height, but she was taller than Emily and Taylor. They both smiled at me.

"Hi, how old are you guys?"

"I am ten," Perry said.

"I am nine, like Taylor. How old are you?" Emily said.

"I am fourteen," I said.

"Wow, you're a teenager," Perry said. "I'm a pre-teen!" She grinned.

"No, you're not! You have to at least be eleven to be a pre-teen. You're still a child like us," Emily said. Perry looked mad.

"It doesn't matter," Taylor said. She seemed mature for her age.

"Well, are y'all excited to go to the facility?" I asked.

"Yeah, except we're mad that those two boys are going to be there," Emily said. She looked at two boys who were a little bit older than them.

"What's wrong with them?"

"All they do is play around, and they are so immature. The shorter one is John Quary. He has attitude problems. The other one just follows him around but is a lot meaner. His name is Andrew. They are so annoying sometimes. They just run around and do what they're not supposed to do," Perry said.

"Have they said anything mean to you?"

"Not really. It's just that when we're eating our lunch, Andrew takes it. John doesn't really do anything." I walked up to the two little boys. They were laughing, probably about something immature. I thought boys were stupid when I was Taylor's age too.

"Hey, Andrew and John." They turned around. They seemed excited that I was talking to them.

"Hello," Andrew said. "What brings you here today?" I think he was trying to hit on me. Gross.

"I hear that you have been taking those girls' lunches over there. Is that true?" I asked politely.

"No, they are lying! I don't even know who they are!" He put a frown on his face. I looked at John.

"Is that true, John?" Andrew was trying to give him a signal. John ignored it.

"Yes, it's true," he said. "We're sorry." He seemed like an honest kid.

"Don't say sorry to me. I want both of you to go over to those girls and say sorry."

"Okay." They went to them and apologized. The girls accepted their apology. They ran back over to me.

"We said sorry," John said.

"Good. Now I don't want you two stealing their food or anything, okay?"

"Okay." I walked to Henry and Alex.

"What was that about?" Henry asked.

"They were bullying those girls, so I made them apologize." Henry and Alex laughed.

"I remember when I was a kid. I never thought girls had cooties, but I was always mean to them," Alex said.

"That sounds like you. It seems like you haven't stopped."

"I'm not mean to you at all," Alex said. I rolled my eyes at him.

"I remember when I was a kid too. I believed that girls had cooties. They would always kick me, though. Until I got in fifth grade," Henry said.

"Aw, poor thing," Alex said. I laughed. I didn't really remember when I was a kid. I just kept walking. I was so bored. I was ready for the walk to be over. I didn't really talk for the next couple of hours. Henry and Alex were just laughing about stupid stuff.

"We are at our final destination for the day," David said. Finally, it was over. I looked up at Henry and Alex. They were ready. I saw Josh, Britt, and Chase go up to David and talk to him. Harold was walking away.

I started to follow him. I turned around to make sure Alex and Henry were behind me. He passed the campfire then went in the opposite direction to where our tents were. I walked very lightly. I tried not to walk fast. Soon there wasn't any clear land. There were a lot of trees.

"Split up. I will hide behind a tree, and you hide behind another one," Alex said. I didn't understand exactly what he meant. Henry hid behind a tree and kept following Harold. Alex went to the opposite side. Each time they would walk, they would get behind another tree. I understood now. I stayed where I was. I hid behind a tree that was right in front of me. Henry and Alex were way ahead of me. Harold was about twenty feet in front of me. I tried running from one tree to another. Soon I wasn't that far from Henry and Alex. Our steps were very light. We tried not to land on any twigs when we stepped. Harold didn't notice us behind him. He didn't even turn around.

There was another tree in front of me. I ran to it but tripped over the root of the tree and fell to the ground. I panicked. My first instinct was to crawl behind the tree. I was going as fast as I could. Still on the ground, I was hiding behind the tree with my legs crossed. My heart was about to explode. I was freaking out. I didn't know what I was supposed to do. I could tell Harold stopped. I didn't dare turn around. I saw Henry. He was signaling me something.

"Do not move," he mouthed. I didn't move. I think I stopped breathing.

"Hello," Harold said. "Is anybody there?" I didn't move. I was still sitting behind a tree with my back against it and my legs balled up.

"Stupid animals," Harold said. It sounded like he started to walk again. I turned to look at Henry. He put his thumb up. I got back up and kept walking. This time I had to move slowly when I went from tree to tree. I could still hear my heart more than my breathing. If we got caught, then we would have died on the spot. Finally, a little cabin was visible. There was another one right beside it. I guess he slept in one of them. The one on the right had two windows. He went into the one on the right. I couldn't see through the window. I ran to Alex and hid behind the tree he was at.

"Can you see what he's doing?" I asked Alex.

"I think he's about to get his towel and stuff to take a shower," Alex said. Henry ran to our tree.

"What is he doing?" Henry asked.

"Getting his stuff to take a shower," I said.

"Oh."

"Good job at falling, Mimi," Alex said, laughing but whispering.

"Shut up. And thank you, Henry, for telling me what to do. At least he's nice, Alex," I whispered.

"I can be nice. That was just funny." He was still laughing, but not too loud.

"It's okay, Mimi. I saw his face. He was freaking out when it happened. He thought you were going to get caught," Henry whispered in my ear. I tried not to smile. I wanted to say, "Aw, he does care about me," but I didn't and wouldn't.

"Shh, he's about to come out," Alex said. Harold stepped out, singing a country song. He had a towel and a bar of soap in his hand. He had changed into different clothes. He went into the other cabin.

"Redneck!" Alex said. "Why did they choose him to be our leader?" *Gosh, he is rude.*

"Someone has to go in there and get his deactivator. He didn't take it with him," Henry said. None of us volunteered.

"I guess I'll do it," Alex said.

"I'm going with you," I said.

"No, you'll be falling all over the place! You're staying right here with Henry." His voice got firmer. He started to walk to the cabin. He opened the door and was in. I couldn't see what he was doing through the window. It was too blurry.

"He's just looking out for you, Mimi," Henry said.

"Yeah, I know." In about a minute, he came back out and ran to us.

"I think this is it." He gave it to Henry. Henry looked at it. He touched the screen.

"It's a touch screen," he said. There was a calendar on the screen that showed day one, day two, and so on.

"We're on day twenty," he said. "It's a Wednesday."

"Yeah, just scroll down to the last day," Alex said. Henry went to the last day. It was day forty. The screen showed, "Day forty: the day of annihilation. At 10:00 a.m. we will start the assignment. Each leader will start off by individually speaking with each child. The alarm system will be deactivated at 7:00 a.m."

"That means we have to leave fast," Alex said.

"How far are we from the road?" I asked Alex.

"I doubt even a mile," he said.

"Good. We will have to be quick, and we can't bring our backpacks. Not even snacks," Henry said. We could hear the water in Harold's shower stop.

"Quick, run back in there and put this where you found it, okay?" I said to Alex. He ran as fast as he could, and I think he just threw it somewhere because he was in the cabin for two seconds and came back out. We ran as fast as we could until the cabin wasn't visible. We slowed down.

"That was quick," I said. Finally we were in clear land. We were at the campfire. I saw that Brittney, Josh, and Chase were still talking to David. David turned around and walked away.

"Nice talking to you!" Britt said. He didn't say anything back. Britt ran up to me. So did Josh, Chase, and Ashley.

"What took you so long?"

"It was a long walk there," I said.

"Did you get any information?" Chase asked us.

"Yes, we will tell you at the meeting! Are all the kids in their tents?"

"Yep," Ash said.

"Well, I guess we will start the meeting now," I said. We walked over to the campfire. Everyone was sitting down. Britt and Ash went to go sit by Josh and Chase. Alex and Henry were right next to me.

"We found out some information," I said. Everyone was staring at me.

"We found out today is day twenty; the last day is day forty. We have twenty days left. They deactivate the alarm on day forty at seven a.m. They plan to kill us at ten a.m.," Henry said.

"That means we have to leave quick," Alex said.

"So what exactly does that mean? Where do we go when we leave?" Jackson said. I had no idea where we were planning to go at all.

"As far as we can from here. Once we find the road, we will just follow it," I said.

"What if they catch us?" Kendall said.

"They usually wake up at eight. That gives us an hour, which means we have to move fast," a guy from the crowd said. He looked about thirteen. He was about the same height as me. I never saw him talk in meetings. There were a lot of people who didn't participate in the meetings. He was sitting by a girl who seemed quiet and shy. It looked like they could be related.

"I'm sorry, what's your name?" I tried to ask politely.

"Jason." He said it kind of quietly. He seemed as though he was nervous. I wondered how I could have been with these people for almost three weeks and still not know all of them.

"Well, you're right. We have to get up early. We can't make too much noise either. Even though their cabin is farther down still," Henry said.

"Does anyone have a watch?" I asked. The girl sitting next to Jason raised her hand.

"What is your name?"

"Liz," she said very quietly.

"Where did you get it?"

"It was in my backpack the first day we got it. I kept it on my wrist all this time." I assumed it had a tracking device on it.

"The day we leave, take it off your wrist, okay? It might have a tracking device on it." She nodded her head. "Also, you're going to be the person who tells us what time it is. So make sure we wake up at around six and leave at seven, okay?" She nodded her head again. It seemed as though she was mute.

"Right now it is nine," she said.

"Okay, well, does anyone have anything to say?" I asked.

"Well, what do we do now?" Kendall asked. She was sitting next to Jackson.

"Now we just keep our cool. Try not to get in trouble or anything. We don't have to be worried for now." I hoped that for the next nineteen days, everyone would just have fun. We didn't have as much to worry about anymore. I was positive we were getting out of here.

"So we really don't have anything to worry about?" Ash said.

"Nope, but someone has to be keeping track of the days," I said.

"I guess I will," Henry said. He was probably the only one who would remember anyway.

"Meeting's over. We don't have to talk about it. Oh, and for now, we don't have to have any meetings. We can just relax," Alex said. He walked to his tent. Everyone just stayed at the campfire and didn't even go to bed. Usually everyone did. I think a big pile of bricks was released off their shoulders. It was still a tragedy, but I think everyone felt relieved that they didn't have to worry anymore, that they were going to be safe.

I saw Henry walking to his tent. I ran after him as fast as I could. I was already kind of out of breath, so it didn't really work.

"Hey, Henry," I yelled after him. He turned around and stopped.

"Yeah?"

"Hey," I said. He just looked at me.

"Um … hi," he said. He had a weird look on his face.

"I remember you said that you were good with electronics. Did you want to go into engineering or something?"

"No, not really, but I had hoped to go to college. I got a scholarship to Harvard Law, but now that's not going to happen." He put his head down.

"It can still happen. Soon we're going to be out of here," I said.

"Then do what, Mimi? We're going to be in hiding when we get out of here. Actually, I don't even know what we're going to do," he said. He sat on the ground, and I sat down beside him.

"Soon this thing is going to be over." I wanted him to have faith. He was in his senior year and was about to graduate.

"You don't know that. Most likely it's not. No one in my family ever went to college. I was going to be the first one. My parents were excited. They were excited because I could make something out of myself which they never did. That's not going to happen now, and it's because of the country we live in. It just wants to add more drama into the world we live in. This is stupid. It's not fair, but neither is life." I was quiet for a while.

"You have to have faith," I said.

"What's the point?" He looked up at me. "I mean, yeah, I am hoping we get out of this like everyone else, but we don't know what's going to happen after we leave this area. We're not going to be surrounded by trees and land. We will be on the road, walking. Cars will pass by and probably realize that we're not supposed to be there then eventually send us back to our leaders, thinking to themselves they did something good, when really they just basically sent us back there to die." His voice got louder. I had never seen this side of him. He was usually happy.

"That may not happen. Alex said that people are finding out the truth about what is going on. People are actually protesting against it and trying to end it. Soon other countries are going to get involved. Maybe everything will be okay."

"Maybe... most likely not. There are a lot of maybes, but we don't know for sure."

"We should think the best, not the worst. If we think the worst, the worst might actually happen. If we have faith that we'll be okay, then we actually might be okay."

"Time will tell." Henry was scared of what was going to happen. He thought the worst, and that wasn't the best way to go. At least, I didn't think so. I never actually thought we were going to die. He did, though. I felt bad for him.

"Well, good night," I said. I walked back to my tent. I thought about what Henry had said. He thought so negatively. Whenever I talked to him, he seemed cool. He didn't seem like he was so... sad. I guess how someone acts on the outside isn't who they really are on the inside. It's just an image. Maybe this whole experience would change a lot of us, but it was just beginning.

# EIGHT

I got a good night's sleep. Everyone else was tired. I guess no one went to sleep until hours after the meeting. Henry was laughing about something with Alex. I remembered all the things he had said the night before. It didn't seem like he honestly felt that way. Maybe he was just scared. I walked over to them.

"Hey."

"Hey, Mimi," Alex said, recovering from laughing so hard. I looked around. Everyone was having fun. It was as though no one had to worry about anything. It was nice that way. I felt someone pull me from my back. I turned around. Ash was looking at me with a big grin on her face.

"Guess what! Guess what!" she said. She had her hands together like a cheerleader.

"What?" I asked. I tried to sound like I was excited. I kind of didn't care since she pulled me away from Alex.

"Chase just asked me out!" she screamed. She was jumping up and down.

"And what did you say?" She stopped jumping and just looked at me like I was stupid. I guess it was obvious what she said.

"Yes, of course!" I didn't get how everyone could try to have boyfriends while all this stuff was going on. It was not the right time at all to be having one. I mean, I was pretty positive we were going to escape, but this was still a serious situation we were in. It was not the right time.

"That's great, Ash!" I tried to sound ecstatic for her. I kind of was in a way. I was happy for her, but she barely knew the guy and we were basically about to get killed, so it didn't really matter. I looked around. No one really cared anymore. No one was worried. Everyone was just trying to have fun while it lasted. No one cared that we had no plan other than getting out of here. We didn't know what our next step was. If we walked, they could catch up to us easily and then kill us on the spot. It seemed like it didn't matter anymore. Britt was walking toward us.

"Did she tell you the good news?" Britt seemed cheerful too.

"Yep." I put a grin on my face.

"Yay! Now we all have boyfriends except you, Mimi," Britt said.

"Right now is not a good time to me."

"Why?" Ash asked. She looked confused.

"Because we are so close to dying and my main concern is trying to live." It was kind of obvious. I mean, hello, we're following these two guys that are trying to kill us.

"Don't worry; we have a plan. Everything is going to be okay. I mean, look around, everyone is so happy." Henry's words were starting to affect me now.

"Yeah, I guess you're right." I still didn't think it was the best time to be thinking of a boyfriend.

"So why don't you find out if Alex likes you?" Britt said.

"I really don't want a boyfriend right now." I walked away. Britt and Ash were trying to tell me something, but then the leaders came to tell us to begin our day.

"Today we are walking more than usual." *Seriously, what is the point? We're walking in circles anyway.*

"Hey, wait up!" Ash yelled.

"Why did you walk away?" Britt asked.

"Because we started to walk." They decided to start walking with me.

"You know, we haven't all walked together since the first day. Actually, we didn't even walk together then," Ash said.

"We haven't really hung out. You've been too busy with Alex," Britt said. I didn't realize that I was excluding them. I didn't mean to. They hung out with Josh and Chase. I rarely ever talked to Josh and Chase. I sometimes talked to Chase, but I guess I made friends with different people.

"Sorry, I guess I just became friends with other people," I said.

"Yeah, people that don't like you," Britt mumbled. Ash elbowed her. I knew what she was talking about. Alex, of course.

"What?"

"Nothing." I pretended I didn't hear her. I didn't want to. She didn't know if Alex liked me or not. He probably didn't, but she didn't have to be rude. I walked faster to get away from her and Ash. I didn't want to be around them.

"Sorry, Mimi, I didn't mean it," Britt said. I ignored her. I wasn't that mad at her, but I didn't feel like talking to her. I decided to walk alone. I didn't know if Britt was still saying anything because I tried to block her out of my head.

I walked alone for the rest of the day. It went by pretty fast. Once we were at the campfire, I walked to Liz.

"Hey, what time is it?" Liz was dragging her backpack as though it weighed a ton. She turned around. At first, she seemed like she didn't know I was talking to her.

"It's eight," she said quietly.

"Oh, okay, thanks." I went to the showers. It didn't take me long to finish. I went to my tent. It was already set up and everything. I could hear someone coming. I really didn't want to talk to anybody, especially Britt.

"Hey, Mimi, are you okay?" It was Alex. He was an exception. I unzipped the tent.

"I'm fine, why?"

"Brittney and Ashley said you were mad." I wasn't really mad at them. I just didn't want to talk to them. I hoped they hadn't told him what they said about him. He crawled into the tent.

"So why aren't you out at the campfire?" he said.

"I'm just tired." I was making excuses to all of his questions. I need to find a different excuse. I really did feel like crap. Maybe I was just having severe mood swings.

"Please come out there." He gave me a puppy dog face.

"I'm fine." *I can't believe I was able to turn him down.*

"Then I will stay." It was kind of awkward with him in my tent. It wasn't zipped or anything, so I could hear and see kids rolling on the grass. They should have been in their tents.

"Okay."

"Okay, really, why are you mad?"

"I'm not." I started to laugh. It was kind of annoying that everyone thought I was mad. I was kind of mad at what Britt said, but not really. I was used to Britt making smart comments. She'd done it since elementary school. Alex looked as though he was going to give it up and stop bugging me about being mad. He rolled his eyes at me. My eye rolling must have influenced him.

"I am so ready to get out of here," he said.

"I think everyone is."

"I heard you and Henry were fighting last night."

"We didn't get into a fight. We were just talking."

"Yeah, and you just stormed off to your tent." He laughed.

"I didn't storm off to my tent! He was being really negative, saying we're going to die. I was just trying to be positive and eventually gave up." It was hard to get through to Henry. He was all negative, saying we were all going to die. That was not my fault.

"That's not what I heard. He said you were all up in his face, saying that you had to have faith or something like that," he said, making air quotes.

"Whatever." I looked away. The kids were still rolling in the grass. I finally saw Ash go over there.

"It's time to get in your tents," Ash told them. I couldn't see their faces, but it looked like the two bad boys, John and Andrew.

"What are you looking at?" Alex asked me.

"Those two bad boys. Well, actually, only one of them is bad; the other one is a good." He laughed.

"They're kids. What do you expect? For them to obey you?"

"They don't have to lie to me in my face. That's what one of them did. He tried to get the other one to lie to me, but he told me the truth. He doesn't get into peer pressure."

"I doubt they even know what peer pressure means."

"So it's a good thing that he knows what's right and wrong."

"You are so motherly."

"Am not!" *I can't believe he called me motherly.* "If you call anyone motherly, it has to be Ash. Always talking about the kids."

"You do too! I remember the first time I talked to you. You said to me, 'We have to take care of the kids.'"

"I didn't say those exact words. I said they weren't able to walk for a whole day by themselves."

"Actually, you did say those exact words."

"Whatever." He always wanted to torment me.

"Okay, Alex, so what about you? You're always saying stuff about me. I feel like I barely know you."

"There's not much to know."

"Please tell me something about you!" I begged.

"I don't really know that much about myself, or at least my family." He was staring outside instead of at me. His face was completely blank. I couldn't read it, but I remembered how he told me he was adopted. He didn't know his parents because they died when he was really young. I figured that he didn't want to talk about it. He put his head back up. He didn't look at me. It seemed as if he was looking behind me. I couldn't think of anything to change the subject.

"Well, I'll just say what I know about you," I went on. "I know you're seventeen. I know your foster parents make less than $50,000 a year. I know you're annoying." He rolled his eyes. "I know you're sweet, generous, outgoing, caring, and … " I didn't want to finish. It might make everything awkward. It was already awkward that he was in my tent.

"And?" he said, waiting. My heart started to beat faster. I was scared to say what I wanted to. I couldn't say it. Instead, I would say something that was also true. He was still waiting.

"I know you are an amazing person." I said it as smoothly as possible. He smiled and then looked away.

"Well, I know that you're annoying too. You take things too seriously." *Oh great, he's just going to say the worst things ever.* "But I also know you are genuinely a good person. You care about people easily, which is a good thing." The tone of his voice changed. My heart skipped a beat. I felt like I was about to pass out. Good thing I wasn't standing. I realized I wasn't breathing. I started to smile because I knew I had a deer-in-the-headlights look.

"Hey, Mimi, we are—" I looked at Britt and Ashley. They stopped when they saw Alex in our tent.

"Oh, sorry," Ash said.

"No, I was just leaving," Alex said. I didn't want him to go. It was nice to talk to him.

"I'll talk to you later," he said. I smiled. When he left, Ash and Britt got into the tent.

"I know you're mad at us right now, but what just happened?" Britt said. They had the hugest grins on their faces.

"Nothing, really. We were just talking." Britt, of course, didn't believe me. I could tell by her facial expression. Ash's grin slowly went down.

"What did you talk about?" Britt asked.

"Nothing, most of the time he was laughing at me and then…"

"Then what?" Their faces lit up like fireworks.

"He told me I was a genuinely good person and I care about people." It really wasn't a big deal. Well, it was to me. I felt like a little six-year-old holding hands with the boy next door.

"That is so adorable," Ash said. She put her hand over her heart and was looking up at our tent. Wasn't she the one saying he was too old for me all the time?

"Maybe he does like you!" Britt said. She was excited. She said the same thing Ashley did.

"Or maybe he just likes me as a little sister, which he has already told me."

"Don't be so negative. If you think he likes you, then he might actually like you," Ash said.

"Whatever you say." I yawned. I was tired, and it was probably only eight forty-five.

"I'm going to sleep, guys." I laid down and closed my eyes, ready for the next day.

# NINE

I was running, running away from the people who were trying to kill me. I couldn't see my surroundings. Everything was blurry. I could hear people yelling and screaming in terror.

"Mimi, we have to go!" It sounded like Alex.

"Come on, Mimi." That sounded like Ash. I walked toward them. Everything was blurry, and I still couldn't figure out who was who. I could picture fire and people running everywhere. It must have been the day—day forty. I followed Britt and Ash.

"Where is everyone else?" I asked.

"I think it's obvious they're running for their lives," Alex said. He sounded angry, not terrified. I tried to get closer to him, but each step I made toward him he ran faster. I stayed next to Britt and Ash. There were people behind me. I couldn't figure out who they were. The fire behind us seemed to get farther and farther away. Maybe we were getting closer to safety.

"We're getting closer to the road," shouted Henry. I just kept running behind the figures I could pick out. My eyes slowly began to come back, so I could see well. I saw Britt, Ash, Henry, Alex, Chase, and Josh in front of me. I turned around, and I could see two angry men coming after us.

"They're getting closer!" I screamed.

"What do we do?" Ash asked, terrified.

"Keep running," Alex yelled. We did, but as we got closer to the road, they got closer to us. We were on the road finally, but they were about two hundred yards away. They were running after us quickly.

"Now what?" I yelled. Everyone was quiet. I looked at Alex. He looked determined.

"You have to go! I will keep their attention," Alex said.

"But they're going to kill you!" I screamed. He knew what he was doing. He was sacrificing his life for us.

"I have to!" He sounded determined.

"No!" Tears fell down my cheeks. "You can't go!" He held my hand.

"I love you," he said. He let go and ran toward the people who were following us.

"No!" I ran to him, but someone was pushing me back. I couldn't move.

"Come on, Mimi, we have to go!" It sounded like Chase. He picked me up and kept running. My eyes were full of tears. It was the last time I would see Alex. I heard a shot. It was more of a *pop*. Everyone stopped running. I knew what it meant. He was gone.

I woke up. My eyes were full of tears. It was just a dream. I got up and went out the tent. I wanted to go to Alex's, but I didn't. I stayed outside and sat down. *What if it really does end up like that? Us running for our lives. What if someone does sacrifice his life for us? What if it is Alex?* He probably would. I would hate for that to happen. But he said he loved me in my dream! In a way, it was one of the best dreams I'd ever had! But I didn't want to think about him dying. I knew if I did I would start to cry. I heard someone unzip a tent. I turned around. It was Alex. He was walking somewhere and then saw me. He looked a little confused. He walked toward me.

"What are you doing?" he asked me. I didn't know what to say, but seeing him made me remember my dream. I tried not to cry or hug him or anything.

"I um … couldn't go back to sleep," I said. "What are you doing?" I asked.

"Same, and I really had to … you don't want to know." I figured he was going to say he had to use the restroom, but he was right. I didn't want to know. He sat down by me.

"So … " I said.

"So why were you crying?" he said. I guess my eyes were puffy. I didn't want to answer him.

"I had a scary dream." I hoped he wouldn't ask.

"About what?"

"It was kind of weird. We were running away, and they caught us. There was fire and all this crap. We were still running, and we got to the road; but the people chasing us were not that far away, so someone decided to try to stall by risking his life and ended up dying." I tried to say it without any details. I also tried not to cry. Thinking of that dream made me want to start.

"Aw, poor thing." He was being sarcastic. "Wait, who died?" No way was I planning on telling him. *He is way too nosy!*

"No one," I said.

"Well, apparently, that no one is why you're crying. Mimi, it was just a dream." I wasn't going to tell him. I stayed quiet. "So who was it?" I still wasn't going to tell him. No way, José!

"I'm not telling you. You will probably make fun of me." I didn't believe that. If I told, he would probably never talk to me again because he would realize that I liked him. "Well, why are you out here? You said you couldn't go back to sleep either, so what was your dream?"

"I don't remember my dreams. They're not a big priority in my life," he said. I rolled my eyes.

"Did you hear Chase and Ash are going out? Now you can stop bugging me about him."

"I stopped talking about it a long time ago."

"Yeah … yesterday."

"Well, I really don't care who he goes out with." It seemed as though he didn't like him. After all that time, he was trying to get me to go out with him. "He wasn't the guy in your dream was he?" Alex asked. He looked up at me, concerned. Ha, no way would it be him.

"No, Alex, forget about it." I was not going to tell him. My heart started to beat faster. I was getting nervous.

"It was him," he said.

"No, it wasn't."

"You're lying."

"No!"

"Yes." I gave up.

"Whatever." I looked away.

"Well, I'm going back to bed." He got up and walked away. I didn't want to be alone, so I went back to my tent. I couldn't go to sleep. Britt was snoring loudly. I tried counting and finally dozed off to sleep.

"Come on, Mimi, wake up!" I was the last to wake up, which bugs me with a burning passion, so I had to shower and get ready quickly. When I was done, we still hadn't left. I walked to Henry and Alex.

"Hey." They looked at me.

"Oh, crap. I forgot something," Alex said and walked away.

"Hey, Mimi," Henry said. He looked nervous.

"Are you okay?" For the first time I asked someone that question. This whole trip I was asked that question. It felt nice.

"Yeah, I'm fine. Aw man, I forgot something too." He walked away. Well, actually, it was more of a run. I had no idea what was going on with those two. I saw Britt and Ash. They were talking with Josh and Chase.

"Hey, guys," I said.

"Hey, Mimi!" Ash seemed really happy. Everyone was losing it today. We finally started walking.

"So you're going to walk with us today?" Chase asked.

"I guess." He gave me a weird look. "Why?"

"Just wondering." He turned around and walked with Ash. Britt walked with Josh. They were behind me. I was just in between them. It seemed like twenty minutes, and I felt a little awkward around them.

"I'll be right back." I went to Henry and Alex.

"I feel so awkward with the two couples over there. They wanted me to talk to them, and now they aren't talking to me. I don't get it."

"Oh, I need to go tell … um … um … Kendall something," Alex said. He didn't even look at me. He just stormed to Kendall.

"Me too!" Henry said. He ran to Jackson and started talking to him. Now I was alone. I didn't know why they kept running away from me. I didn't do anything. Maybe it was that whole discussion Henry and I had, but that was two days ago, and he talked to me yesterday. I went back over to Britt and Ash, who were still walking with their boyfriends. I just stayed in the middle of them, walking alone. Ash and Chase were right in front of me, holding hands. It was adorable, but then again it made me mad. I didn't have anyone or anything. The day was over before I knew it. I was happy about the fact that I could just lie down in the tent not having to talk to anyone, but they were still ignoring me.

I decided to try to talk to Alex again. I left my tent and walked to the campfire. I saw Alex with Kendall and other people. I started to walk toward him and was five steps away when he said, "Well, I'm going to go take a shower," and got up and ran past me without even making eye contact. I couldn't believe this was happening. I didn't understand. He didn't want to talk to me. My lips were dry. My eyes were watery. I probably had a blank face. I just stood there. Everyone was just wondering why I was standing there.

"Yeah, I know you didn't see me coming over here," I said to Alex, even though he was already gone. Everyone was just trying to ignore me. I looked at Kendall. She turned her head toward me. I was pretty sure she saw me but ignored me. She was laughing with Henry and Jackson. I slowly turned around and walked back to my tent. I didn't know what to do. I was just so confused. I wanted someone to talk to, but there was no one. I walked back to my tent and decided to go to sleep.

"Mimi," a shy, familiar voice called out. I unzipped the tent and saw Liz.

"Yeah?" I smiled.

"Well, um…um…I just wanted someone to talk to. I don't really have any friends." Her shy voice cracked when she said "friends."

"Sure, you can come in." She smiled and crawled into the tent like Alex had. She wasn't anywhere near being as tall as Alex. She wasn't even taller than me.

"Hey."

"So are you ready to leave this place?" I asked.

"How can you be so sure we're going to?"

"I have hope! A lot of people aren't worrying anymore."

"Yeah, I guess, but even if I had a plan to get out of here, I would still be nervous." She was nervous all the time, except right now. She was actually talking to me. She wasn't freaking out or being really shy, like most of the time I ever said anything to her.

"I guess everyone will be when the day comes."

"We only have about two weeks left."

"Do you think you're ready?" I asked.

"Yeah, I'm ready to get out of this place."

"That's not what I meant." She was quiet. I didn't understand. "If this doesn't go as planned, are you ready to face the consequences? Are you ready to die?" The words came out slowly. This was a life-and-death situation, and it honestly was scary, but everyone was acting like we were in a movie or something. It was serious, and we were all taking it like they wanted us to take it: as children. Because that's what we were. They didn't kill our parents because they knew they wouldn't be able to get away with it. We seemed like an easy target. The word was getting out, though. I knew people in the world weren't coldhearted. I knew people cared.

"No, I am not ready to die, and I don't plan on dying anytime soon." People were so fed up on dying. We could try to live. Had they all just programmed their minds to "Oh, it's no big deal. We're all going to die"? Or, "Oh, it's no big deal. We're going to survive." What's there to worry about?" In reality, there was a lot to worry about.


It was fun talking to Liz; she was pretty cool once she got out of her shy mode. Alex kept ignoring me. Whenever I was about two steps away from him, he would walk away. I tried not to think about it. Ash and Britt were with their boyfriends. I hadn't really talked to them in a while. Most of the time I walked with Liz and sometimes Jason. I couldn't help but miss my other friends, Britt and Ash. They were my best friends, but the person I missed most was ignoring me and I didn't know why. Guys were so weird. We only had about six days left until the plan to escape. It was actually not that hard—we just had to leave as soon as the alarm deactivated. I decided to go to the campfire instead of my tent. Since all of my friends ditched me, I had been staying in my tent. Liz walked with me. She was shy at campfires. I sat on the ground close to the fire. Alex was there. I tried not to look at him, but I couldn't help it. Why did he just completely try to take me out of his life? It wasn't fair. He was across from me on the other side of the fire. He was with none other than Henry, Kendall, and Jackson. He was sitting next to Kendall. It seemed like they were … together. *I am not going to assume that. There's no way! He said she wasn't his type.* Alex turned his head up to my direction. I looked away as fast as possible.

"Are you okay, Mimi?" Liz said. Even she asked me that on a regular basis.

"Yeah, I'm fine." I looked across the fire to see if Alex was still looking at me. He wasn't.

"Do you wanna go somewhere else?" she asked as though she was concerned about me.

"That would be nice." We got up and walked near my tent. I didn't feel like getting into it. I just crashed onto the ground.

"What's wrong?" she asked. I was getting a little dizzy. I couldn't really move. I crawled into my tent, even though I didn't want to go into it. I fell onto the pillow. That was the last thing I could remember.

"Finally!" Ash said. I had no idea what they were talking about.

"What are you talking about?" I opened my eyes wider. At first, I couldn't pick out anyone. Then I could see all the people surrounding me. Everyone who had been ignoring me was relieved, but I still didn't know why.

"You passed out," Henry said. Alex was right next to Henry. He was just staring at me. I looked toward Britt.

"You were only out for a couple of minutes," Britt said.

"Oh." I was not in my tent. That was the last place I remembered I was. I was outside. I got up, but a rush over took me. I laid back down.

"You're still a little woozy," Henry said.

"Ha … apparently." I looked at Alex. Once he saw that I was looking at him, he went back to his tent. He was still ignoring me. I tried to get up again, this time a little slower. I walked to my tent and crawled into it.

"Good night," Henry and Liz said.

"Thanks, and you too." Ash and Britt got in the tent with me.

"You freaked everyone out, Mimi," Britt said.

"Yeah, Alex was scared. It was his idea to get you out of the tent and let you get some air." That was a shocker.

"That's weird," I said.

"Why?" Ash said.

"Because he's been ignoring me for the past week. Anytime I get close to him, he walks away. After the first day, I gave up on talking to him because he would just make up a lame excuse. I don't know why, but he just stopped talking to me. He doesn't want to talk to me at all! It's not fair." I was lying in the tent. Britt and Ash were about to lie down beside me.

"Aw, I'm sorry. I'm also sorry if you feel like we've been avoiding you too," Ash said.

"No, I understand you guys—your boyfriends and stuff—but the weird thing about it is that I think he might be with Kendall or something."

"Why do you think that?" Britt asked with a weird expression on her face.

"Today they were sitting next to each other by the campfire."

"Calm down; I doubt it means anything. They sit together by the campfire a lot." Wow, that made me feel better. They sat together all the time. He was never that close to her, and now he walked with her every day. He didn't do that with me. I was tired of this.

"I've decided to not care."

"Like that's going to happen," Britt said, laughing.

"No, I'm serious! I don't even want to talk to him. I'm not even going to be close to him." I was dead serious. I was tired of him completely ignoring me. He acted like he hated me, and I was tired of it.

"I hope that works out well," Ash said.

"It will."

# TEN

I was not going to talk to Alex. If he looked at me, I would roll my eyes or something to make sure he knew I was mad. I was tired of him. I didn't hate him, but I didn't like him. I had officially moved on.

"You're so in denial," Ash said, rolling her eyes.

"Am not!" I was serious. I was tired of him and didn't want to talk to him anymore. We were getting ready to walk for the thirty-fifth day Ash and Britt weren't going to walk with their boyfriends today. They decided to walk with me, but I didn't want them to walk with me because they felt sorry for me.

"Sorry, but you are," Britt said. I looked around, trying to find him.

"Ew."

"What?" Britt asked.

"There he is. He thinks he is so amazing. Well, he's not! Ugh ... I don't like that guy."

"Nope, you don't like him at all," Britt said sarcastically.

"I truly don't. He is annoying, and I don't under-stand why I ever liked him in the first place."

"Then why are you staring at him?" Britt asked. I was still staring at him. His head turned around. I was scared at first, but I did what I said I would do. I rolled my eyes, hoping he would know I didn't like him at all.

"Because when you're talking about some-one...um...you have a tendency to stare at them. Duh!" We started walking. I wasn't going to talk or look at him at all. I would try my hardest not to look over at him. Liz walked over to me.

"Hey, Mimi," she said. She didn't sound shy anymore.

"Hey, Liz." I decided to introduce her. "Oh, Liz, this is Ash and Britt, and Ash and Britt, this is Liz." They both smiled. Liz started walking beside me.

"Tell this girl that she's in denial," Britt said to Liz. Liz didn't know. I didn't care. He was out of my life for good.

"About what?" she said with a confused look on her face.

"About Alex. She likes him, but since he's been avoiding her she claims that she despises him." Britt was explaining the story completely wrong.

"I never said despise him. I just don't like him, and I don't want to see him at all."

"Yeah, sorry, but you can't just wake up one day and say, 'I don't like this guy anymore.' It's impossible." Liz was probably right, but I was working on it. I was already to the point where I didn't care about him at all. I was ready to leave, and hopefully he wouldn't be with us.

"How about this? All the girls go one way and the boys go the other. Then we won't have to see them ever again." I was very proud of that plan.

"I'm against it. We won't be able to see our boyfriends," Ash said. Britt nodded.

"Yeah, I'm against it too," Liz said. I groaned.

"Hey, it was a good plan." They laughed.

"Whatever. All I know is we'll be out of here soon … hopefully," Ash said.

"Don't doubt it! They take us for granted."

"Shh!" Ash said. She pointed her finger at the leaders. We weren't that far from them, and we were talking way too loud.

"It is a nice experience, though," I said, just in case the leaders heard me.

"What?" Britt said.

"Getting to meet new people. I never would have met Liz or a lot of other people." It was true; Liz would have still been her shy self. Now she was more outgoing and lively.

"I'm glad I met Chase. He's really nice." Ash was looking up to the sky. She was daydreaming about him when he was right behind us. Britt pushed her to get out of it.

"Attention, we have a break today. It will be shorter than usual, so eat as fast as you can." Harold smiled. He was excited about something.

"Why is it shorter than usual?" Liz asked.

"I don't know, but something isn't right." We all agreed something was wrong, but we didn't know what. We ran to Josh and Chase.

"We think they're planning something," Britt said.

"Like what?" Chase asked.

"We don't know, but why would they make it shorter? Why would Harold smile? He is the crankiest guy I've ever met. He's happy, and the only reason why he would be happy is ... " I thought about it.

"Is what, Mimi?" Ash said. She was trying to figure out what I was thinking.

"Is when we die? What if they changed their plans? What if we don't die in five days or if they don't deactivate the alarm around this area of land?"

"Calm down. We'll have a meeting tonight and discuss it," Josh said. We all nodded. I wasn't hungry anymore.

"Today we have good news for y'all, but I'll wait till we get to our destination." Harold grinned. It wasn't a friendly smile. There was something demented about it. I told a couple of people we are having a meeting tonight. We walked the rest of the day. It seemed like a shorter walk. It wasn't even dark when we got to our final destination.

"Attention, tomorrow will be the last day, and that afternoon you will be at the facility! I can't say how it looks and all they have, but you will find out! Aren't y'all happy?" Harold said. He tried to sound friendly. It wasn't working. I knew what it meant, though. We were going to die tomorrow, but that completely ruined the plan. The days were wrong, or they changed their minds. It didn't seem right. It felt as though the blood stopped running through my veins. It was as if I was frozen in time. All the little kids were screaming and clapping for joy.

"Yay!" I said to make it seem like I was so happy. "My feet are killing me!" Everyone else tagged along. They pretended to be excited and anxious too. Harold and David walked away into the woods. My face went from fake happiness to gloominess. That ruined everything about our plan. I didn't even know what to think. I took a shower and went straight to the campfire. The only people that were already there were Alex and Henry. I sat on the opposite side of them. There was no way I would sit next to Alex. I waited for other people to show up. Finally, Ash came. I didn't see Britt. It was kind of weird because this whole ordeal I had never seen them apart.

"What the heck is going on?" She was terrified. I saw Britt with Liz, and a whole lot of other people showed up. Everyone was there. Ash, Britt, Liz, and I all stood up.

Everyone got quiet.

"Today was supposed to be day thirty-five. They just told us that tomorrow is our last day. That isn't supposed to be for another five days. I don't know what exactly is going on, but I think that we're going to have to wake up tomorrow morning and begin our plan to escape."

"What if it is a trick?" Alex said. I ignored him. I wasn't going to say anything to him.

"I don't think we should go. I think we should stay here," Kendall said. Now her I would reply to.

"They basically just told us, 'Tomorrow we're going to kill you.' It was obvious on Harold's face. I think we need to get out of here."

Everyone was quiet.

"Who's with her?" Ash asked. Josh, Chase, Liz, Jason, Ash, and Britt were on my side, but Kendall, Jackson, Alex, and Henry weren't.

"I still think it's a trick. They might be planning something," Alex said. I looked at him and looked away. I did not even want to see him.

"I don't want to die, so I'm with Mimi," a familiar voice said. It came from behind me.

"Shh."

I turned around and saw John and Andrew.

"What are you doing?" I said.

"We weren't tired, and you guys seem to have all the fun, so we came. Now we're here," John said.

"You aren't supposed to be listening. We were just playing a game. We're not going to die. Now go back to bed!" I commanded.

"Mimi, they're ten. I don't think they're that slow. They might as well know if we are going to leave tomorrow," Alex said. I didn't know why he was talking to me now. It was too late. I didn't want to have anything to do with him, even if I died. I wouldn't want to die with him. John and Andrew walked over and stood right beside me.

"I think we should leave if there is any possible theory that they are trying to kill us," John said. He sounded mature for his age.

"We're with them, so what's the plan?" Andrew said. I couldn't believe it. Those little kids were actually trying to listen to our conversations. At least they were on my side.

"If any of us leave, we're all leaving as a team," Alex said. "So I'm with her too." He smiled.

"Great." I rolled my eyes. His smile slowly turned into a frown. Hopefully he knew I didn't want to talk to him.

"I guess we're all in," Kendall said. I was happy, besides the fact that I had to be with Alex right now.

'So what's the plan?" Ash asked.

"The same thing. Someone has to stay up tonight. Whoever plans to stay awake has to wake everyone up at six. Then we basically are on our way to the road."

"What do we do when we get to the road?" Jackson asked me. I really didn't know. Everyone's mind was blank on that part. We just had to try to stay as far from that territory as possible.

"We have to try to get out of this area as fast as possible," I said.

"I guess I will stay up." Liz said. "I have the watch."

"I'll stay up with you. We'll just stay in my tent."

"I'll stay awake too," Alex volunteered.

"No, it's okay. We have enough volunteers." I smiled a fake smile. He didn't say anything. He just walked to his tent. But I was pretty sure he saw right through my fake smile. Once he left, everyone else did too. Liz followed me to my tent. Ash and Britt were already in there. I knew it was going to be a little crowded with four people in the tent.

"Ash, are you staying awake?" I asked.

"As long as I can, and Britt will too," she said. I was ready for the night to go by fast. We played games at night, but they soon got boring.

"Who wants to play Hangman?" Britt asked.

"We have no paper," I mentioned.

"Well, then, we have to do it mentally," Ashley said. I wasn't good at that, but I loved Hangman. It was fun.

"Okay, I go first. Now since we have no paper, I'll just say each word individually and how many letters are in it. Do you understand?" Britt explained. I got it. We all nodded.

"Okay, the first word is four letters," Britt told us.

"A?" I guessed.

"Nope."

"E?" Liz guessed. Britt shook her head no.

"I?" She finally nodded.

"The second and fourth letters are I," she said. I thought about it. What four-letter word has an I in the second and fourth space? I pictured it. It wouldn't come to me.

"Mimi," Ash said. She was good at Hangman.

"Yes!" Britt said. "The second word is five letters. Since you already said E, the fourth letter is E."

"O?" I said, sticking with the vowels.

"It is the second letter of the word."

"L?" Liz guessed.

"That is the first letter of the word." Britt said. I already knew what it was.

"Mimi loves Alex." I rolled my eyes.

"Ding, ding we have a winner!" She laughed.

"I don't like him. At all! He is annoying to me, and I don't want to be his friend or anything." I probably had said that way too loud.

"It was a joke, calm down," Britt said. "Well, I do believe you still like him, but I didn't mean to make you angry."

"What time is it?" I asked Liz. She looked down at her clock.

"Twelve twenty-one" she said. "We only have about seven hours left." She was happy that we only had a few more hours until we escaped. I was tired. Not really tired, but tired of being here.

"Hey, Mimi, can I talk to you?" My face froze. It was Alex.

"Make him go away," I whispered.

"What did you say?" He had heard me whisper but couldn't make out what I said.

"I will," Ash said. She got up, opened the tent, and stepped out.

"And you say you don't like him," Britt said her arms folded together.

"I don't. I just don't want to talk to him."

"We need to leave her alone about this," Liz said. Liz was the only one not saying anything about me liking Alex. She probably thought I did too, but I was over him. I didn't want to see him or talk to him or anything.

"What is taking her so long?" I looked over at Liz's watch. It was 12:25. She had been out there for four minutes. "It doesn't take that long to say, 'Mimi doesn't want to talk to you.'" Britt was quiet, but I knew what she was thinking. She was probably thinking something like *You are so in love with him* or *You are in denial.* I laid my head down and closed my eyes. They were taking forever. I heard Ash come back into the tent. I opened my eyes.

"What took you so long?" I asked.

"Nothing. He just wanted to talk to you."

"About…"

"I don't know." I felt like Ash wasn't telling me the truth. *What did he tell her? I need to know.*

"Whatever." I put my head back down. I felt like I was drifting to sleep. I tried to stay up, but my eyelids were getting heavy and heavier until it was impossible to keep them open.

I opened my eyes. I was in the same tent. Surprisingly, no one was telling me to wake up. It took a while for my eyes to adjust to the light.

"What time is it?" I asked Liz. She had her back up right beside me.

"Five forty-five," Liz said. Ash and Britt were awake too.

"Sorry I went to sleep."

"It's okay. They stayed awake."

"Should we wake everyone up?" Ash asked.

"I guess." We got out of the tent. My feet were asleep. I stretched before I actually went to anyone's tent.

"I'll go get the kids," I said. I went to Taylor's tent. Her tent was two away from mine. I unzipped it.

"Hey, girls, it's time to wake up." I lightly pushed Taylor and Emily. Perry woke up as soon as I unzipped the tent.

"Why?" Emily said while yawning.

"Today is the special day, remember? They're going to let us walk on our own. Now go to the bathroom and wash your face, but don't be too loud, okay?" They nodded their heads. They got out of the tent and walked to the girls' showers. I started to walk to the boys' tents, but they were already awake. I guess they heard us wake everyone up and never went to sleep. I went to the girls' showers. It was crowded. Ash and Britt were in there. I went to one of the sinks. I didn't notice it at first, but Kendall was right beside me. I washed my face without saying anything to her.

"Hey," she said as I was putting toothpaste on my toothbrush.

"Hey." I quickly started brushing my teeth so she wouldn't say anything else to me. I didn't want to talk to her. I really didn't have anything against her, but I didn't really like her either. I finished brushing my teeth and ran out of the shower. I looked for Liz.

"Liz, what time is it?" I said while running up to her.

"Six fifty." Oh, thank goodness, we were about to leave this place for good. I was so happy. Soon everyone started to get ready. I saw Alex, but I wasn't going to talk to him. Everyone went to the campfire, including the little kids.

"I know which way we go to get to the road," Alex said. "Everyone, just follow me."

"Wait," I said. Everyone stopped and looked at me. "Don't take your backpacks, and, Liz, take your watch off. It could have a tracking device in it," I said. Everyone took their backpacks off their backs, and Liz threw the watch on the ground.

"It isn't that far away from the road," Alex said. He started to walk. I didn't want to follow him. I didn't even want him to be here. We crossed the trail. There were trees everywhere. I had no idea how Alex knew where to go. I hoped I wouldn't trip like last time. I was very careful of my steps. I felt like we were going in circles.

"Are you sure you know where you're going?" I asked Alex.

"I'm positive," he said with confidence.

"I don't think you do," I said. "If we get lost, then what are we going to do?" I was purposely trying to get on his nerves. I was irritated and frustrated with him.

"Do you not trust me?"

"Not really." He rolled his eyes at me. He was getting irritated with me. I didn't care. I wanted to annoy him. He needed to be aggravated. Even though it was a different feeling from what he did to me. He made me feel like he didn't care about me at all. Maybe he didn't.

"Why are you being so ...?" Alex started. "Never mind."

"No, what were you going to say?"

"Nothing."

"Tell me!" I commanded. Not that he would listen to me anyway. He was older than me and was the only way we would get out of here.

"I can't say it right now."

"Why?"

"Actually, I doubt you're even worth it." My heart stopped. I felt so insulted. I knew what that meant. I tried to ignore him, but those words hurt. I decided that I wasn't even going to say anything to him. I didn't want to talk to him at all. I kept telling myself that, but it wouldn't sink in. We kept walking.

"How far are we from the road?" Ash asked. She sounded out of breath.

"Pretty close. We've only been walking for about two minutes." She groaned. We were going uphill. I understood why she was groaning. It was hard. We kept going tree by tree, and I almost tripped on a tree root. All the trees seemed to be right in my face after each step I took. I looked around. No one else was having that problem. I kept walking, trying not to run into anything. I looked at the little kids. They seemed like they were okay. They didn't know what really was going on, but Taylor and all the other girls seemed happy.

I felt something hard hit my face. I fell rolling back. I couldn't hear anyone, but I tried to stop with my hands. The ground felt slippery. Soon another tree hit my back. I groaned because the pain was escalating in my back. I always got hurt.

"Are you okay?" Ash said, frightened for me. It was going away. I tried to stand up, but I could barely get back up. I groaned even more. I felt a sharp pain when I tried to get up.

"I'm fine," I said while groaning. Ash knew I wasn't. The pain was escalating. At first it was going down, but each time I tried to move it got worse. More people started to surround me.

"Come on; we have to go!" Alex said. He was uncaring right now.

"Hello! I can't get up!" I yelled at him. He made me furious. He walked closer to me and put his arm on my back and lifted me up. He carried me as if I was as light as a feather.

"Now come on; let's start walking before they catch us," Alex said. I looked at the little girls, hoping they didn't hear what he said. Thank goodness, they didn't.

I hoped none of the leaders had heard me run into a tree. If they were awake, hopefully they thought it was an animal or something. I decided I wasn't going to say anything to him while he was carrying me. I didn't want to talk to him. He wasn't worth talking to. If only I could let myself believe that.

"You don't have to be so mean," I whispered to him.

"I'm not." I didn't look at his face, but the tone in his voice sounded like he was mad. Maybe because he had to hold me. Suddenly, I could see the road. I hadn't seen a road in a long time.

"Finally," Henry said. It really had only been about a ten-minute walk uphill. We were used to walking a whole day on a trail, so a ten-minute walk wasn't anything. Then again, I was being carried because I hurt my back. When Alex held me in his arms, he didn't squeeze me really tight. It was almost as if I was floating. He was barely even holding me. I wanted to forget about everything. I want to be his friend again, but I doubted that was going to happen anytime soon. We were finally on the road.

"Where do we go now?" John asked. We never really planned what we were going to do once we got to the road. We'd either turn right or left. I looked up at Alex. He was wondering which way we should go. We were doomed. We were just going to end up dying right there.

"Follow the road this way." Alex was still carrying me. We went right. There was finally more clear land. I was used to seeing trees, but on the other side of the road was just land. No trees.

"Okay, so we have no idea where we are going," Chase said.

"You're right, but at least we're out of there," Alex said.

"We're out of there, but now we're stuck here without food, clothing, or anything else. We have nowhere to go!" Chase and Alex started arguing. I decided not to pay it any attention. Henry was right, but out here we had hope. Sure, we were in the road with nowhere to go, but it was better than dying today. I looked out on the road. There were no cars or anything.

"They probably have guards at the beginning and end of this area," I said.

"Let's hope not," Alex said. I didn't look up to see his face.

"I think they might be after us already, so we have to go quick," Henry said.

"Will you shut up and look around? We are on the road, but there are no cars." Everyone looked around and finally noticed what I was talking about.

"That's weird," Britt said.

"Maybe they cleared the roads because they didn't want people passing by this facility," she said while making air quotes and a disgusted facial expression.

"That means that they have it blocked off, and if anyone tries to get in or out, they probably have body-guards surrounding this area," I said.

"Let's not worry about that. We haven't seen anybody yet," Alex said.

"Well, we probably will soon," I said.

"Just don't worry."

"I can worry if I want to." I got a little annoyed with him. Everything he said made me mad.

"Calm down."

"I am calm." He didn't say anything back. He just carried me. I think he was getting tired of me already. I wanted to be able to say I didn't like him, but I couldn't. These might be the last moments I had with these fifteen people. This might be the last moments of our lives.

I heard something. I think everyone did because they all turned around. It was a SUV coming our way. We were all dead. They were after us. I thought maybe we could survive, but I guess I was wrong.

"Should we run?" Britt asked.

"No," Henry said. He looked at her like she was stupid. The SUV was three feet away from us and stopped. I still couldn't see who it was, but it looked like a female. She stepped out of the SUV. She was about my height and had a perfect body for a woman in her late thirties. She had a dark brown hair, not too long, which went with a caramel complexion.

"Get in the car." Her voice was distant.

"Who are you?" Britt asked, determined. I told her not to ask questions when we were getting kidnapped or taken away from our home. She doesn't listen.

"I'll explain when you get in the car." She stood there waiting for us to move.

"You can explain now," Britt said. The lady seemed to get annoyed with her.

"Listen, if you don't want to die, then I suggest you get in the car … now!" Her voice wasn't that loud, but she was getting furious.

"I'll take front seat," Henry said.

"How are we all going to fit in that SUV? There are sixteen of us," Ash said.

"Sit on each other," the lady said. She got back in the car and didn't bother helping us at all.

"Okay, I'll sit in the middle with Britt, and we will have the kids in between us and the girls in our lap. Alex, Kendall, Chase, Liz, Josh, and Mimi, you guys will sit in the back. Chase, Josh, and Alex sit, and then Mimi, Kendall, and Liz sit. Figure out a way to make room," Ash said. Henry was already in the car. He was the only one who had a seat to himself.

"I think I can walk now." Alex slowly put me down. Alex, Chase, Josh, and Jackson sat down with no space in between them.

"I'm glad I have a seat to myself," Henry said with a smile.

"Hurry up," the lady said. I got into the back. I felt a sting on my back. I was in an awkward position. I had to sit on Alex's lap. Liz and Kendall got in the car. I was next to Liz. She was really tiny, so she didn't take up that much space; actually, there was no space at all. Britt and Ash got in the car and had all the kids on top of them. They were packed just like me, but I was worse. I couldn't even move my arms. Britt closed the door and the lady started to go.

"So first off, what's your name?" Britt asked.

"You can call me Ms. Jane," she said politely. Her voice changed a lot when we got into the car.

"So where are you taking us?" I asked.

"To my house. I will keep you in hiding there until this whole fiasco is done and over with. David told me what they were going to do to you. We both decided we were going to save as many people as we could. I told some of my friends, and we started a secret group. They are trying to get other kids also," she explained.

"So that David guy is a good guy?" Britt said.

"I guess you can say that. You guys probably wouldn't have gotten away with half the things you have gotten away with if it weren't for him." Ms. Jane laughed. She was driving really fast. I guessed because the road was clear. She made an exit off the interstate. I could see hotels, McDonald's, Target, and several other places. There were finally other cars. It was nice to see the city again.

"So what's going on in the world?" Alex asked.

"Well, people are finding out about what the government is doing. A lot of people are protesting it. The government was denying it at first, but now they are telling the truth. They're trying to make it seem like a good thing when it's not. It needs to stop," she said.

"Most people in our country make less than $50,000 a year. Are they planning on killing half the population?" Chase asked.

"I really don't know about that, but I do know you have to have certain characteristics to be chosen. Income isn't the only factor," Ms. Jane said.

"What else do they kill you for?" I asked.

"It depends on what type of neighborhood you live in. It also depends on if anybody in your family has ever been charged with a crime. They also see how good your grades are. They find out if your parents have enough money for you to go to college. I don't think the government likes what they're doing, and that's why they get so specific, but I think there's a better solution than killing you." Her tone became more firm. It was as though you could easily tell what type of mood she was in just by the way she talked. She really did care about this war.

"So where exactly are we?" Britt asked.

"No worries, you are still in Alabama. Just in Daphne. It is closer to the beaches," Ms. Jane said.

"Do you think other people are safe?" Henry asked. He stared at her.

"I honestly can't say. I know that some people are going to die. We cannot save everyone and hide everyone, but we are trying." She sighed. I hoped she knew what she was doing. I hoped she could save us. We needed saving to end this crisis in the world. I wasn't really paying attention to our surroundings. I realized we were in a neighborhood. It seemed like each house was a mansion. I had never been around an area like this. She made a right turn. The mansions were a fair distance apart. It seemed as though the mansions got bigger as you went down. We stopped at the biggest mansion, the only house I saw with a gate. The gate was very high up and black. She pushed a button in her car to open it. Her driveway was a circle. She did not go around; she just went straight. The mansion almost seemed like a castle. It was made out of brick, and the house was a pinkish color. Her garage was on the left side of her house. It was a three-door garage.

"Okay, come on; let's get out of the car," Ms. Jane said. First, Henry got out; then Ash and Britt and all the little kids got out. Britt pulled down the seat she was sitting in to let us get out. I got out second to last, with Alex behind me. My back was still hurting. I groaned.

"What's wrong with you?" Ms. Jane asked.

"She hit a tree and then fell down and started rolling until another tree hit her in the back," Britt said. Britt said it like it was nothing unusual. Ms. Jane walked toward me.

"I will take her upstairs, and you come with me," Ms. Jane said, looking directly at Alex. Oh great, I did not want to talk to him. "Everyone else, you can pick out your rooms. Only rooms on the second or third floor." Goodness, this house was huge. She opened the door into the house. Right when you walked in there was a hallway. Rooms surrounded the hallway. Eventually I could see a staircase.

"Do you think you can go up these stairs?" Ms. Jane asked.

"Yes." I took a step. The pain in my back was getting worse with each step.

"I can carry you," Alex offered.

"I'm fine," I said quickly.

We finally were up the stairs. Everyone was following. At the top of the stairs were two rooms that weren't separated by doors. The stairs kind of separated them. In one there was a huge flat-screen TV with chairs identical to movie chairs. It seemed as if it was a movie room or something. We walked past the movie room and were in another hallway. There was a room on the right.

"Here, go into this room and I will be there in a second, okay?" I did as she said. After all, she did save my life. I walked in with Alex behind me and closed the door. I guessed she was going to tell them where they could and couldn't go. The room was painted sky blue. It was a pretty big room but very empty. There was a king-sized bed with dark blue pillows and a light blue comforter. Next to the bed was a dresser with a lamp on it. I figured she never went into this room. It wasn't dusty, though. I laid on the bed without saying anything to Alex. My back was stinging like crazy, but I tried not to show any pain with Alex there. It was awkward for several minutes, and then Ms. Jane came into the room.

"Hey, sorry I took so long." She looked out of breath, like she had been running. "Now what's your name?" she asked me with a bright smile on her face. I was pretty sure it was a fake smile because she didn't even know me.

"Mimi," I said.

"And yours?" she asked Alex.

"Alex." He smiled at her, trying to be polite I think. She turned back toward me.

"Now turn around and let me see your back," she said. I didn't notice she had a first-aid kit in her hand. I turned around on the bed. Ms. Jane walked toward me and pulled up the dirty shirt I was wearing. She gasped.

"Your back is completely scraped up." She opened her first-aid kit and got out rubbing alcohol and two cotton balls.

"No, please don't! I hate rubbing alcohol. It stings like crazy."

"It won't hurt at all."

"Can't you use peroxide?" I shouted.

"I don't have any." I started to whine like a little baby. I was trying to stay under control, but it was hard and she hadn't even started yet. "It will only take a minute," she said.

I closed my eyes. I didn't want to see anything. All of a sudden I felt liquid on my back. At first I didn't feel anything, so I opened my eyes. It started to sting out of nowhere. I was screaming with my mouth closed. She was rubbing it all over my back. It felt like she was burning my flesh away. I closed my eyes again, trying not to move. I could still hear Alex laughing even louder.

"Shut up!" I yelled at him. He didn't stop. She stopped rubbing the alcohol all over my back. It was still stinging.

"I'm going to put some Neosporin on it, but I have to find it first. I'll be right back." She left the room. I turned back around and pulled my shirt down from my back.

"You're like a little baby." He was still laughing. I didn't show any emotion. His face went from a smile to a frown. "Are you mad at me?" He looked clueless. How could he not know I was mad at him? I rolled my eyes and didn't say anything. I heard Ms. Jane walk back in.

"Here you go!" She was a very bubbly person sometimes. When we first met her, she was very stern. Now she was all happy. She put the Neosporin on my back and then gave it to me.

"I want you to stay in the bed for the rest of the day." I didn't complain. I had to obey her. She was the only person I knew that cared. I nodded my head. "I'm sorry, but I think it's best for you." She gave me a sad face then walked out. Alex stayed in the room. I hadn't noticed there was a flat-screen TV in the room. I turned the TV on. I completely ignored Alex.

"You didn't answer my question," Alex said. I glared at him for a second and then looked back at the TV. I couldn't find anything to watch, so I just kept switching channels. All of a sudden, he grabbed the controller out of my hands.

"Are you mad at me?" I finally had to talk to him. It stopped at some stupid paid program.

"I think the answer to that question is obvious." I didn't give him any eye contact. I didn't want to look at him while I was being a complete jerk to him.

"Why?" He was really clueless.

"Why do you think?" I still didn't look at him.

"I haven't done anything." He was lying to himself. I was pretty sure he avoided me on purpose, and I was pretty sure he knew what he was doing. I didn't say anything to him. He was acting stupid, but then I remembered he had the remote control.

"Think really hard, Alex. I mean, it's not that complicated. Did you start to avoid anyone or just completely try to erase them from your life?" My voice accidentally got louder. He was quiet. He knew what I was talking about.

"I'm sorry." He got next to the bed and bent down. "I didn't mean to avoid you."

"Yeah, right."

"Okay, maybe I did, but I didn't mean to hurt you." I still wouldn't look at him. Of course it was going to make me mad. I was furious about it.

"How did you expect me to take it?"

"I hoped you wouldn't care. You acted like you didn't care."

"Of course I care! You were my friend, Alex." I finally looked at him. His face was usually content, but right now there was something different about it. He wasn't the happy, fun, annoying Alex. He looked as if something was bothering him.

"I'm sorry that I hurt you." His voice sounded gloomy.

"Why did you avoid me in the first place?" I asked. He was quiet. At first, it seemed as though he didn't want to answer.

"I don't know. I guess I didn't want to be around you." My heart sank. I looked down. My eyes were getting watery, but I wasn't going to let the tears fall unto my face. He noticed the change in my expression. "Sorry, I worded that wrong. What I mean to say is that I didn't want to be friends with just you. I wanted to hang out with other people. I'll explain later. "That didn't really make me feel better.

"Whatever." I rolled my eyes at him. I really need to work on that.

"I am truly sorry, and I hope you will forgive me." I looked at his face. He looked genuinely sorry, and usually he was never serious. Even if he was kidding around, I probably wouldn't be able to turn him down.

"I forgive you," I said. He got a smile back on his face.

"So we're friends?"

"I guess." He hugged me.

"Ow, my back." I groaned

"Sorry," he said.

"It's okay. So what's been going on with your life?" I asked him. He looked at me as if he didn't know what I was talking about. "Lately you've been hanging out with Kendall and them. Do you like her?" His expression didn't change one bit. He still looked confused.

"No, I mean, as a friend but not any more than that," he said.

"Aw, I thought you two would go out." I smiled. Maybe he felt that this wasn't the right time to be with someone. Thank goodness someone was actually sane around here. He stepped back and looked around. I didn't know what he was looking for until he finally sat down in a chair.

"What about you and Chase?" I was hoping he was going to stop talking about him.

"You need to leave that alone. He goes out with my best friend. I never liked him anyway, so I really don't understand why you're so obsessed with him."

"What about that dream you had about him?" He wasn't making any jokes at all. He was completely serious, which was weird.

"Are you okay, Alex? You're acting different." He looked at me.

"How?"

"You're not usually so serious or dull; most of the time you are making annoying jokes about me."

"Well, I'm just tired. Anyway, you didn't say anything about that dream." He used my excuse. Now I knew something was up. I was going to leave it alone, though. *He is so stupid. The dream was about him.*

"Goodness, Alex, he wasn't the guy in my dream, and just because I had a dream that someone died and cried about it doesn't mean that I liked the guy. It could just mean that I really cared about the person as a friend." I knew eventually I was going to have to tell him who it was.

"So you had a dream about another person?"

"That's what I have been telling you for over two weeks." It fit together. He was mad because he thought I liked Chase. That's why he stopped talking to me. "Wait a minute. The reason you stopped talking to me was because of Chase? You thought I liked him? But why would you ignore me because of that?" *I am so good.*

"That's not true." He didn't look at me at all when he said that. I was going to leave it alone. It was probably wrong anyway. He had been trying to make me go out with him for the past four weeks.

"Whatever you say."

"It really isn't completely why, but you still haven't told me who it was." He was determined to find that out.

"Gosh, Alex, it was you!" Although I liked him, I didn't want him thinking I did. I looked at his face. He looked kind of shocked. He tried not to show it.

"Aw, I didn't know you cared." He was finally being his sarcastic, annoying person again.

"Shut up." I rolled my eyes. He laughed. I wanted to change the subject. "So do you think we will survive the next step?" He got quiet.

"I hope so. I'm glad we are here, but I don't know what's going to happen."

"Same. I am glad the trail is over."

"The trail might be over, but this is the beginning of everything." He sounded kind of sad.

"I don't know. This is better than anything else. We would have died."

"I know. That's why I am okay for right now. But what about tomorrow or the day after that? Right now, we might feel safe. But we're not. No matter what, they're going to keep killing until people become outraged."

"When people are outraged and fight against it, this is going to end."

"People thought the Civil War was going to be over in a month or so. It ended up lasting four years, and I don't even know how many people died."

"What's your point?"

"My point is that you may think this will end in a week or so, but it could take a year and thousands of people could die." He was right. It wouldn't be over just like that. It would take some time, but hopefully it would be over soon.

I got out of the bed slowly and started to walk. My back was still bruised, and Alex helped me walk. We went into the movie room, where everyone was playing around. They seemed happy. Even at a time like this, they can be able to feel happiness. I didn't know what would happen in the next month or even the next day, but we would get through it. I looked up at Alex. I had a feeling he was thinking the same thing.